never too MUCH

www.chellebliss.com

CHELLE BLISS

USA TODAY BESTSELLING AUTHOR

Publisher © Chelle Bliss September 3rd 2024
Edited by Lisa A. Hollett
Proofread by Read By Rose & Shelley Carlton
Cover Design © Chelle Bliss
Cover Photo @ Wander Aguiar

CHAPTER 1
BENITO

"BENITO, get inside. You're going to catch your death."

I try to shake the rain from my hair, but it doesn't matter. I'm drenched. I'm pretty sure my raincoat hit its saturation point about two hours ago, but that's what I get for trying to save a few bucks by taking the delivery guys off the schedule.

"I'm all right." I wave my hand at Rita, the hostess who acts like she's the one who owns this restaurant, not me.

She clicks her tongue, and all five-foot-nothing of her huffs to the front door. "You're the hardest working man in Star Falls, but this is too much. You're going to make yourself sick."

There's love under her motherly warning. In fact, Rita prides herself on being an honorary mother to everyone who works at Benito's. Which means I not only have to put up with my own smothering mother, but I have one at my restaurant too.

"I'll take you home tonight," I tell her, wiping the back of my hand over the raindrops dripping down my face. "Lights are out across town, side streets have puddles deep enough to swim in. You're not driving."

Rita wags a highly polished fingernail at me and then points toward the parking lot. "You think I drove myself? With the forecast we had?"

I look through the glass door and see the headlights of the station wagon that belongs to Rita's much-younger boyfriend. And by much younger, I mean seventysomething to her eighty.

"Thanks for the offer, sweetheart, but I have a ride home." Rita rests her bottom against her stool and carefully slips on her rain boots. "And if I'm lucky, I'll have a ride *at* home too." She twists her glossy red lips into a pucker and blows me an air kiss.

I chuckle, trying not to cringe at the image of Rita getting lucky back in the senior community where she lives. "Anybody left inside?" I ask while Rita gathers her purse and umbrella.

"One at the bar," she says, "and there's a couple at table ten." She lifts a hand up to pat my cheek, and I bend down so she can actually reach me. She grips my chin in still-strong fingers. "Now you go dry off and get some rest," she tells me.

I grin at her and hold the door while she opens her umbrella. But before she can protest, I grab the flimsy handle from her and tuck her protectively under my arm. I angle the thin black fabric, pointing the tip of the umbrella into the wind, trying to keep it from flapping the wrong direction and leaving us both exposed to this brutal storm.

I hurry her through the buckets of rain pounding against the paved parking lot until we finally reach the passenger door of the waiting vehicle. I yank open the door and see Samuel, whose big smile glimmers under his bristly white beard.

"Benito," he says, the windshield wipers running on high speed, a measured rhythm that feels predictable and comforting. "Good to see you."

I nod at Samuel, holding the umbrella against the pouring rain while Rita climbs into the car. Once she's in, I close the umbrella, shake it off, and set it beside her boots in the footwell. "Get home safe," I say, then close the door and hoof it back toward the restaurant, trying not to skid and fall on my already-wet ass.

I meet a couple coming out just as I'm going back in. This must be my couple from table ten, so I wish them a safe drive and watch as they duck their heads and hurry toward their car.

I flip the small sign on the front door to Closed, lock the dead bolt, and blow out a hot breath that leaves a tiny mist of fog on the glass. If I have one more customer at the bar, I'll want to make sure he's able to get home safely before I let him out.

I shake my arms, covering the floor with water from my raincoat, and head toward the bar.

"Jesus. You need a towel?" Maggie, my kitchen manager, spots me before I even make it five feet into the restaurant.

I shrug. "I'm all right, Mags. Everybody else go?"

She tosses me a look. "Of course. You told us to close the kitchen early. You think I need to tell those heathens twice?" She chuckles, then gives me a wave. "I'm out too, now that you're back. Jasmine's up front at the bar, but once she sees you, I'm sure she's going to take off. You're good to lock up?"

I nod. "Drive safe."

She nods. "Will do." She jerks a thumb toward the kitchen, and her expression grows serious. "Benny. You remember about tomorrow?"

I tug down my hood and stifle a groan. Truth is, I remember nothing. So much goes into running this place, and Mags is my right hand. She could mean I'm meeting a new bread vendor or that we have a fire system inspection. I don't have a freaking clue.

"Refresh me?" I say, bracing for Maggie's ire. She's been riding me hard the last few months—and with good reason. I've been running like a chicken with my head cut off. If Mags didn't put food in front of me, I'd probably forget to eat most days. Not a good look for the head chef and owner of his own restaurant.

"Jesus, Benito." Her brows, lips, and tone make me feel ten years old again, although my parents would never invoke Jesus when scolding me. Ma still keeps a swear jar in the house even though all her kids have grown up and moved out, and my Italian parents aren't that religious, but we don't take anyone's name in vain if we can help it. Mags doesn't seem to have that same concern, because she's muttering something I can't make out under her breath. Finally, she frowns, her words sharp as a paring knife. "This is important, Benito. You know we need that grant."

Fuuuuck.

The grant.

"Right, yes. I know, I know, Mags. I got it." I nod, trying to reassure her that I do remember and that I will take this thing seriously. I don't tell her I'll have to dig for the email she sent me weeks ago to remember what *this thing* even is.

Mags and I have a very different opinion about what this business needs. The problem is, I'm a short-term thinker, and she's got vision, which means, in this case, I know she's right. I've got to make more of an effort to see things her way, but before I can say anything, she huffs at me and heads back toward the kitchen.

"Mags," I call out. "Mags, I'll go. I'm going to go."

She stops but doesn't turn back to face me. "Tomorrow. Nine thirty in the morning. You got the address?"

"I got the address." Well, I probably do. Somewhere in my emails or maybe in my texts. I'll find it, and I'm not going to piss off the best employee I have by admitting I only think I know where it is. "Thanks, Mags."

She heads back toward the kitchen to clock out, and I sigh. Without Mags's anger and Rita to worry about, I can finally release some of the tension in my shoulders. The warmth of the restaurant starts drying my damp hair, although my toes are an entirely different story.

Star Falls is a beautiful place to live every day of the

year, but when Mother Nature decides to whoop our asses, she doesn't play around.

The rubber soles of my boots squeak on the tile as I pass from the front of the restaurant toward the dining room. I can see there is someone still seated at the bar, but it's not a guy, as I assumed. In fact, from what I can see of her back, the blonde cozied up to my bar looks young. Almost too young.

I toss the bartender, Jasmine, a questioning look, but it's lost on her. She gives me the same shocked frown that Rita and Maggie did. "Did you swim to make all those food deliveries?" she asks.

"Just about," I sigh. "You got any coffee made, Jas?"

She shakes her head but offers to make some.

"Nah." I wave my hand. But then I point to the woman on the barstool. "Unless you'd like some for the road?"

At my words, the customer turns slightly on the barstool to face me. I can see right away she's not underage. The crinkles around her eyes when she grins at me assure me she's at least my age. I'm relieved, though I never doubted Jas. She's got a seventeen-year-old son at home who got busted for underage drinking at a lake party this past summer. She grounded his ass for three whole months. I trust her to bring that same mama energy to my business and not serve anyone who isn't legal, even if the whole damn place is empty now.

The woman on the barstool sucks her full lower lip into her mouth and squints at me. "Coffee for the road?" she repeats. "Is that your way of telling me the kitchen's closed?" She softens her words with a grin.

"I'm not from around here, so if I'm overstaying your hours…I can take a hint."

Jasmine glares at me and sets two empty mugs on the bar. "You're fine," she says to the woman, giving me a look that I'm sure means something. But right now, I'm too damn wet and cold to interpret my bartender's silent messages. "I'm going to make some coffee. He needs it, even if you don't."

Jas busies herself filling the pot, and I motion to a stool a couple down from the woman. "You mind?" I ask. "No need to entertain me. I've been running deliveries for hours. I'm dying to get off my feet."

My customer waves a hand in silent invitation for me to sit, then she pats the stool beside her. "I wouldn't mind some company."

I shrug out of my wet jacket before laying it over a stool and taking the seat beside her.

I roll my neck and grimace a little when the joints crack as I work out the tightness. I heave a tired sigh, then shove the wet hair back from my face. "New to town, you said?" I ask.

"Here for business," she says, turning a little on her stool.

I look up when Jas sets two steaming mugs of coffee in front of us, along with a condiment caddy containing sugar and creamer.

"Thanks, Jas. You out of here?" I ask, directing the question to my employee.

"You bet your behind I'm out of here." Jasmine motions to the coffeepot. "Be a doll and turn that off before you go? I'll clean it when I open tomorrow."

I nod and then look to the woman beside me. "Jas is about to go. You can stay and finish your coffee. No rush. But if you want anything else…"

"I closed out my bill already," she interrupts, giving me a smile. "But I'll pay cash for the coffee."

Jas already has her purse over her shoulder and her jacket on, tucking her hair under the hood. "Coffee's on the house," she calls, knowing I won't mind. "Everybody get home safe."

After she bustles away, I shake three packets of sugar into my coffee and roll the tiny paper envelopes between my fingers. It suddenly strikes me that I'm famished. I worked through the dinner shift and haven't eaten since lunch. That feels like it was days ago. I reach for one more sugar—even if that only means a couple more calories, I'll take them.

"You know," the woman beside me says, breaking the sudden quiet, "far be it from me to criticize because the meal I ate tonight was absolutely fantastic…"

My gut tightens at her words. I'm braced for the "but." Embedded in that compliment is *something*. A searing critique of my small-town Italian eatery. The outdated carpet. The renovated home with a slightly kitschy vibe that gives Benito's its family atmosphere. I'm a fantastic fucking cook, but I'm a one-man show. I do the orders, the inventory, staffing, training, and, like tonight, I even fill in for deliveries when I have to. And while this woman can't know I'm hanging on by a thread here, I am. She can't know that, but whatever she has to say, I'm sure as hell not in the mood for it.

"Go on," I say, forcing my tight voice to loosen a

little. She has no idea who I am. No idea I own the place. That the name on the front sign is me. I could just tell her I'm off the clock, not interested in talking about work. But she's a customer, so I grip my mug a little tighter, take a sip, and wait for whatever critique she has.

She reaches past me and grabs the rolled-up remnants of my sugar packets. "A sugar sifter would be more eco-friendly. Less packaging. Less paper waste."

Huh?

I wasn't expecting that. She could have insulted the decor, the food… But I can't exactly sniff at a sustainability suggestion. To be fair, shit like that—small cost-saving measures that are good for the environment —are on my long list of things to do. They're just so far down the list, I don't know if I'll ever get to them.

"Great idea," I say, trying not to sound like I'm dismissing her. "Although that would mean there would be all these little plastic condiment caddies going to waste. What's worse? Paper in the trash or plastic?"

She opens her mouth to say something but then just looks me over, as if she can't decide whether I'm fucking with her or not.

"I'm kidding," I say lightly, giving her a smile that I hope will distract her from any more comments about how I run my restaurant.

She swivels her stool so it faces me and crosses one slim leg over the other, the tip of her sleek boot slightly grazing the damp leg of my jeans. "I'm Willow," she says, thick brown eyebrows narrowing as she studies my face. "Nice to meet you."

I set down my coffee and rub my hands together to

warm them. "I'm Ben," I say, giving her a shortened form of my nickname. If she associates "Ben" with "Benito," as in the name painted on the front door, she doesn't show it.

We shake hands, holding on to each other a little too long at the end.

After our introduction, I realize how quiet the restaurant is. The sound of the rain hitting the roof and splashing against the windows is soothing.

This is my place. My restaurant. The place I've built from the ground up, and while it's a chaotic life, it's mine. This place and the people who work here are everything I care about. Everything that makes me who I am. Well, after my family, that is.

I'm enjoying the quiet and the stillness after the rumble of the furnace kicks off, when the woman beside me lifts the mug to her lips and takes a deep sip. "Can I be honest with you?" she asks.

The low vibration of her sensual, confident voice curls around my ears like a whisper, but it also hits me like a ton of bricks. I'm not sure if she is hitting on me, is lonely, or is just looking for a little conversation. But damn, my body takes notice of every inch of her as she leans toward me.

Her eyes sparkle, the gray almost identical to the stormy skies outside. Her face is free of makeup, but the feature I am most transfixed by is just inches from my face. This woman's top lip has sharply defined peaks, but the lower lip is full and soft. She's nibbling it between her teeth, a playful smirk on her face.

"You want to be honest?" I repeat, warming inside

when I meet her eyes. "Star Falls is a small town. If you plan on staying for any length of time, you'll find out trash talk travels faster than this storm did. I'm not much for gossip, so go for it. Speak your mind." I point to the condiment caddy. "Unless you plan on trying to talk me out of putting sugar in my coffee. Then I'd tell you to take your opinions and…"

She's grinning at me like she's known me forever, and she reaches over to touch my arm. "And what?" she presses.

I smile, relaxing into the light touch on my arm. "Let's just promise to keep things honest. Now, lay your truth on me."

She grins again, the flush on her cheeks brightening her whole face. "Have you had the kale ravioli?" she asks. Her voice is so full of quiet enthusiasm, it's like she's asking me if I've got the combination to the safe and she's a bank robber.

I nod, trying my best not to preen. The kale ravioli is my signature dish. It's colorful and rich, nutty and satisfying.

I know it's good.

I know I'm good. But I'm more than happy to sit here and listen to her say it.

"Mm-hm," I mumble. "And?"

She rolls her eyes back and flutters her lids closed. "That," she says dramatically, "was one of the best damn dishes I've ever eaten. I may just have to try to copy the recipe."

I look her over, a swell of pride lifting my chest.

"You liked it?" I ask casually, acting as if I'm bored,

even though I know I'm shamelessly baiting her for more. "You had the kale?"

"I loved it," she says. "The perfect balance of comfort food and elevated dining. Totally unexpected."

Her light blond hair is pulled back into a ponytail, the long end resting on the curve of her right shoulder. She's wearing black jeans that barely reach the tops of ankle-high black boots. Her turtleneck is white, and I find myself scanning the front of it to see if she has any droplets of sauce to prove that she actually enjoyed my signature dish. I'm not sure I could eat a great pasta dish —let alone an exceptional one—without spilling at least a few drops on myself.

But as soon as my eyes travel to the front of her body, I realize I look like I'm checking her out. She catches me, her face studying the movement of my eyes over her figure, but she sure doesn't look like she minds.

I have a reputation around Star Falls for being a ladies' man. I've had more than my fair share of bartenders and waitresses walk off the job after spending the night with me and finding out that one night together did not make us *a couple*.

But Willow is hot and seems uninhibited. She hardly knows me and yet is pouring on the charm. I'm either much sexier drenched by the rain, or this woman is hard up for companionship. I'm not sure I care. It's been a long day and a very long time since I've had a night of fun. If I'm reading the signs right, she might leave my restaurant with a lot more than a memory of the best damn meal she's eaten.

"I'm not in town for long," Willow says, resting her

palm on her knee when we finally pull our hands away. "What's fun to do in Star Falls?"

The truth is, I don't have a damn clue what's fun anymore. I work, sleep, and occasionally fuck. I'm thinking that very thing when I feel a gentle nudge against my arm.

"Say it," she urges. She's smiling at me, the curve of her upper lip begging to be sucked. I can't resist a beautiful woman, but the more I look at her, the more I can see this woman is not merely attractive. She's confident and assertive. She's a stranger in town, alone at a bar, and she's most definitely flirting with me. I'm sure of it now. And I'm not about to let a torrential rainstorm put a damper on this flame.

"Say what?" I ask, drawing out my words and grinning.

"Whatever you were thinking," she says, a tease in her voice. She runs a fingertip along the lip of her coffee mug and cocks her chin at me. "The look that you had on your face was seriously naughty."

"Naughty," I echo, shaking my head. "Yeah, it was."

"So…" she urges. "Come on, Ben. What were you thinking? What's fun to do in Star Falls?"

I sip the last of my coffee and set the mug back onto the saucer. I chuckle. "Honestly," I tell her, "I was thinking all I do is work, sleep, and occasionally fuck. That's what I do for fun."

"That's perfect," she says, leaning toward me. "Because I was about to ask who I have to fuck to get a copy of that ravioli recipe."

CHAPTER 2
WILLOW

I DON'T HAVE a five-year plan.

I have a one-year rule.

And that rule is never, ever stay in one place for too long. There is so much freedom in living with a finite horizon ahead. It's made me fearless in the face of so many things that scared me. Offered me peace when everything around me felt like chaos.

And when it comes to getting what I want, there is no better motivator than the one-year rule.

How would your life change if you knew with every certainty that you would be someplace else, surrounded by a whole new group of people, doing something totally unique, at the end of one year?

You can damn well bet that you wouldn't sit around and wait for anything.

Not for the promotion. Not for a call from some guy. Not for anything.

So much can happen in one short year, but if you sit on your bum and stay in place?

I won't ever let myself get stuck that way.

Never again.

I'm one week into my one-year experiment in Star Falls. This is my last night in the hotel before moving in to the condo my company has rented me for the next twelve months.

I had no intention of hooking up with anyone when I finally made it to the little Italian place everyone in Star Falls raves about. I can't even remember the name of the restaurant now… Bruno's or something. I've been working nonstop and have so many restaurant names in my mind and so many people to meet, it's all a bit of a blur.

What are the odds that I'd meet a hot delivery driver on a cold, rainy night? The only thing waiting for me in my hotel room is a *probably* stale half bottle of Chianti and a vibrator that most definitely needs to be charged.

Our banter is fun.

And when he stands up from the bar to turn off the coffee, he gifts me a glimpse of his ass that has me rethinking my usual safety protocols. He's tall, dark, thick, and funny.

Exactly my type.

But since I am not about to end up the lead story on a true crime podcast, I need to pump the brakes just a little.

While he clears away our mugs and stands to lock up the restaurant, I pull my phone from my purse and text my friend Jessa.

Me: Met a hot guy. May take him back to the hotel. You've got my location?

Two seconds later, I get a row of thumbs-up and celebration emojis.

Jessa: Send me a picture… And be safe.

The little text bubble appears and then a second text.

Jessa: I'll call the cops if you don't text me in two hours. Where are you again?

I message her back, remind her Star Falls, Ohio, and promise to check in. Then I thank my lucky stars that she's on bed rest and staring at her phone with very little to do.

You'd think with a one-year rule, I wouldn't have a lot of friends, but the opposite is true. I've found that the ones who really matter stick around in my life, no matter where the road takes me. New York, Nashville, Austin, Omaha, Monterey… I've lived everywhere and belong no place. But I have so much love in my life from dozens of friends I've met along the way.

Star Falls may be three time zones away from Jessa, but if she didn't answer, I have two dozen other close girlfriends who'd have my back. Maybe not as immediately as Jess does, but she is sitting three times zones away, cooking a baby who might decide to come months too early if Jessa so much as lifts a finger.

I text back, imagining the stack of paperbacks and adult coloring books I shipped her last week sitting on her bedside table, then turn my attention back to the hometown hottie.

Me: Love you. Feet up and tits out. Cook that baby until well done.

Ben dims the lights in the restaurant and nods at my

phone. "You need a ride? Might be tough to get a rideshare at this hour, especially in this weather." His smile is sincere, almost apologetic. "Small-town living."

My car should be arriving along with the rest of my furniture on the truck that's bringing it sometime this week. After I spent nine months in Monterey, a few months shy of the one-year rule, my company decided it would be cheaper to put my car on a flatbed than to have me drive it from California to Ohio in late October. Weather delays and storms like this could have set me back. Time that I would have been stuck in hotels instead of working on-site here in Star Falls.

I reach for the rain jacket that I hung on the purse hook under the bar. "I walked, actually," I tell him. "I'd better bundle up." I set a few dollars on the bar top. "Will you make sure the bartender gets this?" I ask him. "For the coffee."

He nods, looking from me to the dollars and back again.

"You know…" He tugs his rain jacket over his arms and shivers slightly. He must be cold and damp, and I can't help thinking I'd like to warm him up in my walk-in shower. "We don't know each other, but I've got a mother and a sister who would sauté my balls for breakfast if I ever let a woman put herself in harm's way. I'd be happy to drive you so you don't have to walk."

I hop down off my barstool, and he comes to stand beside me. Our height difference is almost comical, and he must see that. He chuckles and shakes his head.

"Scratch that. You wouldn't be walking. That wind

would scoop you right up and blow you all the way to your hotel."

I press my lips together and consider his offer. "You delivered dinners tonight? Out in this weather?"

He nods, studying my face. "I did."

"And did the meals all make it safely?"

He looks at me again, a thick, dark brow lifted slightly in question. "I'm extremely good at what I do," he assures me, a confident grin on his face. "Pizzas and pastas all made it to their destinations, toppings intact."

I nod. "If you can be trusted with ravioli, I think you can be trusted with me." But I hold up my phone. "I do have location tracking on my phone and a load of friends who will be expecting to hear from me. So, no serial-killer shit. We clear?"

"No serial-killer shit," he promises, his grin wider now. Then I feel his hand on my lower back. "You *really* liked that ravioli." He says it almost as an afterthought, but I stop in my tracks, my boots silent on the carpeted flooring.

"I never joke about food. I live for it," I tell him.

His smile grows even bigger, the heat of his palm spreading a ripple of warmth through my raincoat. "Then you are most definitely in the right hands."

Holy shit.

Talk about the right hands.

Ben's wet clothes are piled in the corner of my bathroom, the steam from the water fogging the mirror.

While he warms up in the shower, I'm in front of the vanity, digging through my overnight bag for a condom. After the things this man did to me with his fingers… I want more. So much more.

Hence the need to strip down, warm up, and move from the lumpy sofa in my hotel room to a more comfortable spot.

I wrap a towel around myself and check the time. It's only been an hour since Ben brought me to my room, helped me finish off that half-bottle of not-stale-after-all Chianti, and we made out like teenagers on a very sad-looking sofa. I have at least another hour before I need to check in with Jessa, and I plan to spend every minute of it wisely.

I grab a foil packet from my toiletry bag and then hang my towel neatly on the hook. Ben is under the hot water, his eyes closed and his dick just beginning to go soft.

We can't have that…

I open the glass door, step carefully inside, set the sealed foil packet on the ledge beside the little bar of soap, and point to the showerhead. "Would you angle that a bit?" I ask.

He nods and reaches over my head. "Like this?"

The hot water hits the back wall of the shower, a little bit of the spray still keeping us warm and wet. I nod, grab a washcloth, drop it to the tile, and then I carefully kneel on it.

"Willow…" He groans as I line up my face with his cock.

My hair is wet and hanging around my shoulders in a waterlogged mess, but I don't care.

Ben is beautiful. His thighs are dense with well-defined muscles, dark hair covering his strong calves, arms, and the divot between his tight pectorals.

He's even got cute guy feet, which is saying something. I can't remember hooking up with many men whose toes I noticed in a good way, but his are actually really, really cute.

I smile as I cup his balls in a hand. "This okay?" I ask, humming the question low in my throat.

"Fuck yeah." His eyes are closed, and he looks like he needs something to hold on to, but the shower stall is huge.

"Shoulders," I say, peeking up past the erection that is slowly coming back to life to catch his eyes. "You can lean on my shoulders if you need to."

His throaty laugh is rich and deep, and it sends shivers along the fine hairs on my arm. "I don't want to crush you," he says. "Not while my balls are in your hand. I'll stand here as long as you need me to, babe."

I grin and lick my lips, then lower my face to his cock. I lick long, wet strokes along his shaft while I gently graze the underside of his balls with my fingertips.

"Fuck… Willow…" My name is silk on his lips as the hot water runs in little rivulets through his chest hair.

I suck him into my mouth, swirling my tongue. When I feel him go completely hard, I point toward the condom.

But Ben's oblivious, his eyes closed, his lips lightly

parted. So, I gently slip my mouth away from his dick, and that gets his attention immediately.

"Condom?" I ask.

"Fuck yes. Sorry. Shit, that felt good." He reaches for it, but then he reaches a hand out to me. "Come here," he says. He grabs my hand in the one that isn't gripping the condom and tugs me to standing. He lowers his face to mine and brushes his lips over mine. "Have you ever had good shower sex?"

I breathe in the warmth of his face, nuzzle my nose against his damp skin and slightly stubbled cheeks. "Hmmm… No, actually."

He wraps his hands around my waist, the condom tucked between two fingers. "Move someplace dry?"

I lift my mouth to his and cup his face, pulling him close for a kiss. He flicks my upper lip with his tongue, and I open to a deep, searing kiss. A kiss that brings my hips tight against his, the heat of his erection pressed flat against my belly. I moan low in my throat, a rush of electricity buzzing from my lips to my core. "Dry," I agree, meaning where I want to go—and not me. Because this man has me wet and aching.

He switches off the faucet, and I grab my fluffy towel, then hand him a clean, folded one from under the sink. We dry off quickly, and I'm shocked by how comfortable and easy this is.

He shakes his wet hair like a dog after a rainy walk, and I rub my long, wet strands between the ends of my towel so they don't drip.

We're on top of the bed, towels on the floor, seconds later. I'm on my back, and Ben is on top of me, kissing my collarbone and running his hands along the muscles of my thighs.

"Willow." He breathes my name against my bare, still-damp skin. "What do you like?" He lowers his mouth to my breast and flicks his tongue against my nipple. "This?" he asks, his voice low and raspy, just before he clamps his teeth lightly around my incredibly sensitive peak.

My hips buck slightly, and I suck in a breath as sparks shoot from my breasts through my body. "Oh, that. Yeah. That's good. So, so good," I assure him. "You can be rough with me."

A little whimper slips from his throat at my words. "Like this?" he asks, devouring my breast with his mouth. He sucks hard on my nipple, his tongue finding just the right speed to work me into an aroused haze.

"Yes." I arch my back, straining to bring more of my skin into contact with his heat.

He withdraws his mouth and rests his chin lightly on my chest, then he cups my breasts between his hands and slowly moves his head from left to right. He somehow—and God, I wish this room had a mirror so I could watch him do it—is able to hold my breasts together and rub the stubble of his chin against my nipples until the sensitive skin is nearly raw.

My legs tremble with need, and I open my eyes when he lifts his mouth from my skin. "Do you like being fucked hard, Willow?"

He's staring into my eyes as he asks, and for a second, my heart jumps in my chest. He's so, so beautiful. "Yeah," I say, stroking his stubble with my fingertips. "Fuck yeah. But I'll only come if you're behind me."

"Then I'm going to fuck you that way," he promises. He kneels on the bed, tears into the condom, and sheathes his incredibly rigid cock. Then he motions for me to roll onto my stomach.

Before I'm even comfortable, his hands are on my ass, kneading my cheeks, and he's planting hot kisses along the backs of my thighs. "Ben," I pant, arousal flooding between my legs. "That's so, so good."

I half expect him to plunge into me and go hard, but Ben is not like other hookups. He takes his time, nudging my legs apart, then lifting my hips so I'm kneeling on the bed, my ass in the air.

"Can you breathe?" he asks, and I feel his hand swipe the wet clumps of my hair away from my face.

I peek at him over my shoulder and grin. "I'm good," I tell him. "This is perfect."

I try to stay kneeling as he nudges the tip of his cock against my entrance, but Ben doesn't just drill in and start pounding. He takes his sweet time stroking his head along every wet inch of my pussy. I chirp a little sound when his dick rubs against my clit. He slides his erection through my wetness, teasing every bit of my drenched seam until I drop my face to the comforter and practically smash my ass against his hips, greedy and needy for all of him.

"Ben." I want him inside me. I'm so, so close to coming. He's primed my body to the point that when I feel him grip my ass cheeks and slide inside me, I see stars behind my closed eyelids. "Fuck." I gasp and widen my knees as far as I can, while kneeling to let him go deeper.

"Good?" he asks. "You going to come for me?"

I whimper a yes into the bedding and let my body melt into the pleasure. He thrusts slow and deep, then fast and hard, then back to slow and steady.

My ass is so high in the air, I can feel the moment he hits that spot inside and my body takes over. I move a limp arm between my legs, press back into his thrusts, and hold my fingers over my clit. Between my fingers and his cock, I'm lost, spinning, spinning, crying out, and collapsing against the bed, my legs too weak to hold my body weight up.

He is careful when I lie facedown not to smother me, and he kisses my back and shoulders while I sigh through every second of my postorgasmic bliss.

"The noises you make," he growls against my ear. "Fuck, Willow. I almost came just hearing you."

I swallow against the dryness in my mouth from all the panting and moaning, and I shimmy my hips so he knows I want to roll over. He moves the massive weight of his body off mine, and I flop onto my back. "I'll scream as loud as you want if it'll make you come," I say. I lift my face to kiss him, then settle onto my back and open my legs. "Come on, gorgeous," I tell him. "Your turn."

My phone buzzes and jolts me from the orgasm haze that has me half asleep. I squint open an eye and feel

Ben's arm against my chest. We're under the blankets now, and I have no idea what time it is. I grab my phone and see two texts from Jessa.

Jessa: Bitch, it's been two hours. You have exactly ten minutes to check in before I'm making that call.

And then, two minutes later:

Jessa: Willow, you better be having one hell of a good time. You have eight minutes to let me know you're okay before I call the cops.

The last text came in five minutes ago, so I quickly thumbs-up her message so she knows I'm alive, then quietly try to text without waking Ben.

Me: I'm great. Alive and safe. Having fun. Luv u.

I hit send, and then silence my phone because I know she's going to want all the details. And right now, I have to figure out how to wake my delivery driver and send him on his way.

I set my phone back on the bedside table just as Ben huffs a deep sigh and tucks himself tighter against me. He's sound asleep, like, not just post-orgasm snoozing. His lips are parted, his damp hair curling over his forehead, and he's now got both a leg and an arm thrown over my body. I'm on my back, and I adjust the pillow beneath my head as best I can around the mass of man on top of me.

I consider waking him, thanking him for a good time, and sending him back out into the elements. I don't know if he lives far, has someone waiting for him at home—a wife, a kid, a dog, even. But something tells me that the man who was so attentive, so conscientious about bringing me pleasure, doesn't have a deep, dark secret or loved ones he's abandoned at home.

I could be wrong, but I dismiss those thoughts and close my eyes, letting the last little bits of bliss wash over me. It won't be too long before he probably wakes up and slips out. Right? I just close my eyes for a second because this man feels *good*. I don't believe in long-term plans, but there's nothing long-term about just one night. Won't do any harm to rest like this for a few minutes…

CHAPTER 3
BENITO

WHEN I WAKE up with a desperate need to pee, I realize in shock that I am not in my loft that overlooks a gorgeous view of the river. I'm even more comfortable than I am in my own bed, and that's almost more shocking.

I look down at the naked woman tucked against my bare chest—the reason I'm so damned cozy here.

Somehow, after fucking each other into next week, we're still stuck together. Willow's air-dried hair is splashed across a pillow, her plush ass pressing into my rapidly waking cock.

I drop a kiss to her hair, and she stirs lightly but doesn't wake up, so I climb out from between the covers, trying to disturb her as little as possible. I pad over to the bathroom, shut the door, then turn on the light. My clothes are in a wet heap on the floor, and fuck if I don't wish I could steal a bathrobe and drive home in something dry. The thought of pulling those clammy

clothes back on and going back out into the storm…
Sigh.

But there's nothing worse than a hookup that
overstays his welcome. After I take care of business, I
hold my breath and pull on my clothes, stifling the
curses that threaten to slip out. Freaking rain. I manage
to wiggle into my freezing-cold clothes, then I click off
the light and head back into the room to find my wallet
and phone.

As I pass the bed, I notice Willow is awake. She's
tucked the blankets up to her chin, and she's watching
me move through the dark. We don't say anything, but
as I slide into my shoes, something stops me.

I'm suddenly overcome by the desire to stay. To
crawl right back into bed with her and go for round two
—and then maybe go back to sleep. Through the muted
light of the hotel room, I can just make out her eyes
following me.

After my boots are on, I walk over to the bed. "Hey,"
I whisper. "You awake?"

"Mostly," she murmurs. I can make out her smile,
even in the dark. "You taking off?"

As tempted as I am to stay, I nod, then lean down
and brush the hair back from her face. I plant a light kiss
on her lips, then her forehead. "You stay in bed," I tell
her, but before I can pull away, she reaches a hand from
under the blankets and laces her fingers through mine.
Wordlessly, she brings my hand to her lips and kisses the
back of it. Then she lets go and turns over, snuggling
down into the blanket.

I'm confused by the gesture. It's not an invitation to come back to bed, but it's tender and sweet.

I walk to the door, flip the dead bolt, and then realize once I leave, she'll need to get up and flip the extra locks. "Willow," I whisper, but my voice comes out louder than I intended. "Are you going to get up and lock this behind me?"

She's quiet for a moment, and then I hear the rustling of blankets. She walks completely naked through the room, and as soon as I see the faint light seeping through the curtains from the parking lot and land on her body, my cock does its best to convince me that I don't really have to go home. Her nipples are hard, and the memory of them in my mouth almost has me reaching for her. This was a perfect night, and I can't break the unspoken rule of hookups.

Never let it mean too much.

Never overstay.

Never assume.

Fuck, done, and run.

She runs a hand along my arm and grins at me through the darkness. "Goodnight, Ben," she says gently. It's not a dismissal. In fact, she sounds a little reluctant, like she's thinking about inviting me back to bed.

"You'll lock this?" I ask, reaching for the doorknob.

"I will," she assures me, her fingers tightening on my sleeve. Holding me back. Tempting me to consider staying. That means this is most definitely my sign to go.

My clothes have fully brought my body temperature down, and if I don't get my ass onto my heated seat, I'm going to start shivering. I open the door a crack because, after all, she's totally nude, and quickly step into the hall. Before I walk away, I block the doorway with my body so no one who might happen to pass by at this hour can see in. "You know where to find me," I tell her, giving her a nod.

"Bruno's," she whispers. "Best kale ravioli ever."

I almost choke on my laughter, but instead, I just shake my head, a grin on my face. "Benito's," I correct. "And it's the best *damn* kale ravioli ever."

We trade smiles, and for a moment, neither one of us moves. But then, I hear the ding of the elevator down the hall and figure she'd better shut the door before she flashes an unwitting housekeeper or guest.

I nod, wait for her to close and lock the door, then I head toward the elevator and out into the night.

———

I'm awakened the next morning by banging and shouting.

"Fuck." I turn over in bed and jam a pillow over my head to muffle the noise. But I can still hear what sounds like giants bowling in the hallway outside my condo. I squint and grab my phone, about ready to call the property manager to send someone up to deal with this shit, when I notice the time. It's after nine.

I have ten text notifications on my phone, but I am sure half of them are from Mags reminding me where to go, so I don't bother reading them. I jump out of bed and bolt into the bathroom, mentally calculating how late I'll be if I skip making coffee.

I fucking hate skipping morning coffee.

I hate rushing.

I hate being late.

All of this because I got home at three in the damned morning after…

The steam is fogging my bathroom mirror when I remember showering last night with Willow. Her body, her lips, her dripping hair. The way she squirmed and moaned as I rammed inside her.

Fuck.

If I had even five more minutes, I'd jerk one out just to ease the pressure building in me at the memory of her.

Willow.

I know she's new in town, but I didn't even get a last name.

I lather up fast, trying to wash the feeling of her from my body. It's weird; it's like my body is still with her. Like I can still feel her limbs tangled with mine. I put my whole head under the spray and try to push away the memories.

Once I'm out and dry, I brush my teeth and throw on a pair of black jeans and a dress shirt, then check the forecast. Cloudy, but no rain. I don't think my rain gear is anywhere close to dry yet. I tuck into a pair of boots, grab a thick zip-up cardigan, and yank open my condo door, only to practically fall over a moving crew.

"Hey." One of the guys nods at me. "You got your new neighbor's number? We're scheduled to do a move-in today at noon, but this was a cross-country move, and we made it ahead of schedule. Any chance you know where she's at?"

I scowl. I didn't even know I was getting a new neighbor. I shake my head. "Sorry, man. I got to run."

The new neighbor explains the noise, but it's barely nine thirty. It'll be a miracle if I make the SBA event before it's over. And I'd rather embarrass myself in front of the entire Star Falls Small Business Administration than face Mags if I blow this off.

I bash on the elevator button, but it must be jammed with shit from the movers because I wait a whole minute before turning and bolting toward the stairs. I take them two at a time, tucking my phone into my sweater pocket so I don't drop it.

I literally run to my truck and pray the traffic light gods look favorably on me.

"I've been a good boy," I mutter. "I could use a little positive mojo right now."

As I navigate through our small town, my phone rings. I see who it is on the caller ID and smash the button on my SUV's display screen.

"Ma, I'm in the car, and you're on speaker."

"Benny?" Ma's voice sounds concerned. "Honey, why am I on speaker?"

I roll my eyes. "Ma, I'm not just sitting in the car. I'm driving. I'm talking hands-free because it's the law now. You know this. What's up with you?"

Ma launches into an update on her morning—she's good, my father's in Cleveland at a doctor's appointment. "He wouldn't let me go with him, Benny," she finishes.

I partially tuned Ma out while she was chatting me up. She often calls me on Monday mornings, while my brothers and sister are working or off taking care of their kids. I'm the youngest of four, and all of my siblings have partners and kids, so I'm the only one around during the weekday mornings when Ma `wants to catch up.

"Wait, wait." I can't tell what time it is since my phone and my display are showing me the time I've been on this call, but it's got to be quarter to ten as I pull into the very full parking lot of the Star Falls Community Center. I park in a spot at the far end of the lot and grab my phone. "Ma, what'd you say about Pops? He wouldn't let you go with him to the doctor?"

I turn off the engine and slide out of the car, tucking my phone between my shoulder and my ear. My parents do everything together. They have slept apart only a handful of times since they got married, and they met when they were fifteen. Pops doesn't buy a slice of cake without Ma approving the flavor and amount of frosting. I can't believe he'd drive into Cleveland for even a routine doctor's appointment and not take Ma with him.

"He told me not to worry, Benny, but you know that means I'm going to worry. Are you still in the car? You sound funny."

"Ma, I'm… Do you know what kind of doctor it is?"

We have great primary care here in Star Falls, but for surgeries and more serious stuff, most people go to one of the major hospitals in Cleveland.

A sick feeling creeps up the back of my neck. Fear,

maybe. Anxiety? My parents are still young, but hell, youth doesn't guarantee good health.

Our family has been spoiled in that department.

My mother's explaining that she has no idea and that she's even considered snooping on my father's phone to find out, but they've never had that kind of marriage. I listen as much as I can, but when the doors of the community center open and a dozen people head out into the gloomy morning toward their cars, the dread in the pit of my stomach deepens.

"Ma, Ma…I hate to interrupt, but I—"

I'm trying to talk over her, but I'd have to shout over her, and right now, there is nothing more important than this. There is nothing more important than my family. So, I shut my lips and listen to Ma talk. No matter how pissed off Mags is going to be at me for blowing this meeting. I made my bed last night when I fell asleep in the arms of a gorgeous woman instead of going home early and setting my alarm. Looks like I'm going to have to lie in it.

By the time Ma and I end the call, I'm back behind the steering wheel. I turn over the engine and head into downtown Star Falls. If I'm going to be on Mags's shit list, I might as well bring a peace offering. I park in front of the bookstore café and squint to see if Ma's there yet. Of course she is. And she's not alone.

I yank open the front door and shout, "Yo-yo, Ethan."

My sister's son immediately jumps up from a toddler chair and runs to greet me.

"Uncle Benny."

I pick up the little rat and smooch my lips against his soft ear. "You reading already? You're way too little to be reading, E. You're like a teeny tiny baby."

Ethan curls his upper lip, playing along with the game he never gets tired of. "Not a baby," he growls. "I'm a big boy."

"Yes, you are." I set him on his feet, and he takes my hand and pulls me toward the counter, where my mother looks worried.

"Benny." She opens her arms, but instead, I open mine and fold my mother against my chest. In her stacked heels, she's still ridiculously short, but her highly sprayed dome of auburn hair just tickles my chin when I lean down close to kiss the top of her head.

"Ma." I give her a squeeze, then nod at the front counter. "Where's Chloe?"

My eldest brother Franco's wife Chloe owns the bookstore café and normally runs the place with some part-time help. Especially unpaid part-time help like my ma. We all love it. Lucia never worked outside the home, but now she helps care for her grandbabies or her kids' businesses. She's so involved in our day-to-day lives, she doesn't have time for anything that's just hers. Except for my dad. And he's the reason I'm meeting her here for coffee.

"I told Chloe you were on your way. She ran back to grab some peanut butter crisps to go with your coffee." Ma blots under her eyes with her fingertips, careful not to poke her eyeballs with her long, perfectly manicured nails. The color of the day is navy, and little glittery gems are glued to the polish, which perfectly matches Ma's gem-studded jeans, silver boots, and navy top.

I scan the bookstore, looking for anyone else who may be listening. Ethan's back in the children's reading nook, plastic trucks and board books scattered on the colorful braided rug.

"Gracie working?" I ask, nodding at my nephew.

"Not yet." Ma points at her watch. "I've got Ethan until we pick up the big kids from school."

Gracie works at the tattoo shop just a couple of storefronts down from the bookstore. She's probably enjoying a few minutes of alone time while her husband's kids from his first marriage are in school and her toddler Ethan is here with my mother. My brother-in-law is an early bird, so he's probably been at work since seven.

I rub my face, realizing the hell I'm going to pay when I get to the restaurant. But this is where I need to be.

"Benny." Chloe comes bustling from the back room, a white paper bag and two large coffees in her hands. She drops everything on the counter, then comes around to give me a kiss hello. We're a touchy-feely family, and even though Chloe's one of the newest members, she's taken to our smooches and hugs like she was born to be a Bianchi.

"Hey, kiddo." I give her a quick squeeze. "How's my dickhead brother?"

A sudden slap against my bicep reminds me Ma is standing right there. "Benny. Language."

I chuckle and shake my head in apology. "Sorry, Ma." Then to Chloe, I say, "How is my d-head brother?"

Ma snorts and gives me another good whack while Chloe just flushes pink. She's used to the way we play in this family. I grab the white paper bag of peanut butter crisps, and she slides one of the coffees across the counter toward me. "So, should I mention any of this to Franco?" she asks, sounding concerned.

I look to Ma. "What do you think? Is this family-meeting material, or are you just venting until Pops gets home?"

My mom sniffles and blinks her heavily made-up eyes. "Let's just keep this between the three of us for now," she says. "I'm hoping your father tells me everything when he's home, and then we can all put this worry behind us."

My mouth goes dry as I think about the alternative. I'm so used to my parents being there whenever I need them—and even more often when I don't need them. We used to do weekly Sunday dinners, but now that all of my siblings have kids and spouses of their own, Sunday dinners have become monthly events, not weekly.

I miss the old days when we ate together every week, just me, Ma, Pops, Gracie, Franco, and Vito around the table. But things change. Families expand. Kids are born, and our parents...well, they grow older. Whether we're ready for it or not.

I clear my throat, pushing away the emotions before I start blubbering like one of the kids. I grab the coffee and the bag, lean down to kiss Ma goodbye, and nod at Chloe. "Text or call me, Ma," I say before I leave.

She nods at me, the sadness in her eyes and the dragging down of the corners of her lips nearly breaking my heart into pieces.

After I leave the bookstore, I walk up to The Body Shop and peek in the window. I know it's closed. It's too early for them to be open, but there's something about knowing that my sister will be here in a couple hours that brings me comfort. Everywhere I go in town, there are reminders of my family. The garage where Franco works. The fire station that's Vito's second home.

Some people grow up wanting to leave the place they were born, but not me. Star Falls is my home. Always has been. Always will be.

That's why I opened my own restaurant, even though I had plenty of offers after culinary school. This is what I want to do, where I want to be.

It's just a shame that things change.

It's not enough anymore to make the best kale ravioli in town. I need to up my game at the restaurant.

I'm drowning in paperwork, but who has time to get organized when we're open seven days a week?

The building I rent for the restaurant needs a new roof, but under the deal I signed, I'm responsible for improvements and maintenance to the place. It seemed like a great deal six years ago when I opened the doors.

Now, with a roof that won't likely make it another

winter, life is piling on, and I'm not sure I can handle one more stress.

I pull into the empty lot of my place and thank God that Mags's car is not already there. I'm going to have to eat some serious humble pie.

She's going to be pissed I missed that meeting. I get an idea and pull out my phone. I pick out a small bouquet of flowers from the local florist. I don't have Mags's home address on me, so I think the better of it. I can't exactly send her flowers to the restaurant, or people will think something's going on between us.

Shit.

But there is someone I wouldn't mind seeing again. Someone whose last name I don't even know. I delete the order I started for Mags and pick out a bigger bouquet of tasteful flowers instead—nothing that screams "I'm a stalker in love." More like, "I'm a classy dude who had fun fucking you last night and would love to know your last name." I fill out the delivery instructions, including the room number and her first name. That should be enough for them to reach her. On the card, I type out:

Not as good as the kale, but… Thinking of you. B

I include my cell phone number, pay for the order, and slip my phone into my pocket. Then I peek inside the bag and count the peanut butter crisps. I'm going to need every one of them to stay on Mags's good side.

CHAPTER 4
WILLOW

WHEN I CHECK my phone after my presentation, I see a dozen missed calls from a number I don't recognize. I grimace and am just about to check my voice mail, when a young woman from the audience confidently approaches me.

"Excuse me? Ms. Watkins?" The woman's smile is friendly, so I slip my phone back into my purse and give her my full attention.

"Hi." I hold out my hand, and we shake. "I'm Willow Watkins, but please, call me Willow."

She nods. "I'm Maggie Tempestini." She motions to the rows of folding chairs behind us. "I, uh, was hoping my boss would be here today, but he must have gotten —" she frowns "—distracted."

I nod, sensing tension there but choosing not to comment on it. "Well, I'm glad you made it. Are you interested in the SBA grant?"

She nods again. "I manage a local restaurant with strong ties to the community. We're family-owned, not corporate, and the owner trains and employs a lot of people with nontraditional backgrounds for careers in food service. Our oldest employee is in her eighties, and we have two bussers with developmental disabilities," she says with no small amount of pride. "We make great food, and our people are treated very well, but the owner…" She bites her lower lip, the only glitch in her well-practiced speech. "His heart is bigger than his head."

I've heard that so, so many times before. I conjure a vision of the countless restaurants like the one where Maggie works—the owner pulled in a thousand directions, things falling through the cracks. "Let me guess," I say softly, leaning a little closer. "You badly need kitchen upgrades? You're behind on vendor payments or rent?"

She shakes her head, and a hand flies to her throat. "No, thank God. No. It's our roof. We're renting the space, and we're responsible under the lease for replacing the roof. I know Benito thinks we can make it another couple of winters, but the grant you're offering would get us there so much faster."

I break out into a grin when she says Benito's. "Do you work at the local Italian place? Killer kale ravioli?"

Maggie's mouth drops open, and she raises her brows. "You know about us?"

"I ate there last night," I tell her. "It's one of the few places people won't stop telling me about." I think back to the faded carpeting and Mom's basement vibes that passed for the place's decor. Benito's was homey and inviting, not unlike dozens of restaurants like it across the country.

Maggie claps her hands. "So, maybe since I know you loved the kale… You did love it?"

I nod, a vision of a very naked busboy's bare ass pressed against the glass wall of my hotel shower clouding my memories of the meal. I choke down a cough. "I did. I absolutely loved it," I assure her.

"Well then, maybe—" Maggie clasps her hands together "—you can let me know what we need to do to have the very best chance of winning the grant?"

This, too, happens every year. The company I work for, Culinary Capital Partners, goes into cities and small towns after running the numbers. We evaluate a region's demographics, infrastructure, socioeconomics, and lots of other variables. Then we select a market that appears ripe for a new restaurant or chain expansion opportunity. I've worked for the last eight years on the development side. After our numbers team makes the internal assessments and recommendations, we determine the type of restaurant most likely to be viable in that space.

We then lease or buy property, complete the renovations, do all the hiring, and open the doors with a very aggressive goal for the establishment breaking even within the first two years after opening. By year three, a majority of Culinary Capital restaurants are profitable. I get involved in the very critical period before the doors are open. Once we establish a site and a plan for the restaurant, I move in to the town for six months to a year to oversee the on-the-ground operations. My job is part general contractor, part bookkeeping, part HR, and all about the food. It's why I love doing what I do.

Culinary Capital does a lot to give back to the communities. We're a for-profit venture, and we do know how to make money. We're selective about everything, and I have to be a bulldog on the ground, making sure construction or renovation costs stay on deadline and within budget. I recruit chefs and court discounts with vendors that ensure every project is a winner for the company's bottom line.

But inevitably when we move into a town, the restaurants already in place suffer. A glossy new eatery will inevitably drive away customers, and sometimes struggling restaurants aren't able to compete with the new, shiny place in town. Businesses have closed; people have lost their jobs. It's the hard reality of doing what we do. In order for us to make money, sometimes, others lose it.

To offset the very bad blood that would otherwise exist between us and the food community in the cities we go into, I started a grant program, normally administered by the local small business association.

The grant varies in amount by region and location, but any restaurant that might be impacted by our move into the market is eligible to apply for a no-strings-attached grant. Some of the grant recipients take the money and send their head chef to a special training program, so they can expand their menu or modernize their food handling practices.

In some communities, restaurant owners have hired chefs with no formal training other than basic state-mandated sanitation and food safety. I know of at least three chefs who were able to attend culinary programs paid for in part by a Culinary Capital grant.

The amount of money we're making available to the food service community in Star Falls is not small, so I'm not surprised that Maggie is here, trying to figure out what she can do to make Benito's application more competitive.

I give her a smile. "I won't play favorites," I tell her, "and I don't make the final decisions myself anyway. As I shared in the presentation, we work with the local SBA so the community that will be impacted by the grant has a say in who receives it." I lean close to her and give her a smile. "But how about I come into Benito's again this week and have a chat with you and the owners. I'd love to hear more about the place, and maybe I can give you some tips on how to write a strong proposal."

She grins so wide, she looks about ready to bounce on her heels. "Thank you," she breathes. "Thank you so much, Ms. Watkins."

"Please, call me Willow." I pull a business card from my portfolio, hand it to her, and jot her name and cell number down in my contacts. I confirm when she's on shift and try not to feel guilty for having some ulterior motives behind my offer. It'd be nice to see the sexy delivery driver again, assuming he'd be anywhere I might find him. I lucked out on a rainy night to catch him at the end of his shift, inside the restaurant.

It occurs to me then…

"Maggie," I ask, curiosity getting the better of me.

"Is Benito's just the name of the restaurant? Or is there a Benito who runs the place?"

I hope my cheeks aren't flushing. This is ridiculous. I'm a grown woman who has every right to hook up with a man I find attractive. I only hope he was a busboy and not a man whose restaurant might apply for a Culinary Capital community development grant.

"Oh yes," she says, rolling her eyes. "You'd have met him if he'd have shown up like I asked him to." She seems to catch herself midsentence, stopping the next words from running out of her mouth while she blushes hard. "Benito is… Well, he's an amazing chef. And a larger-than-life ego. He's just—"

I hold up a hand, cutting her off. "No need to explain. I've worked with hundreds of restaurant owners in my career. You don't get to be in that position without having a lot of…let's call them quirks."

She looks relieved, and I want to reassure her that she hasn't said anything that's going to damage Benito's shot at the grant. I'm only one of the people on the committee who will review the applications. I'm not in charge of the final decision, but still.

As Maggie bounces through the now-empty meeting room toward the parking lot, I hope against hope that I don't have to recuse myself from the committee entirely because I fucked a hot restaurant owner my first week in Star Falls.

I smother a grin and pull out my phone to check my messages. That would be a first, and I don't know how I'd explain to my boss my reasons for pulling out. But as I think back to Ben's mouth on my breasts, his cock slamming deep inside me, I hope against hope that Ben isn't *the* Benito.

I tuck my phone beneath my ear and head toward the parking lot to wait for a rideshare, listening to the voice mail from the strange number.

"Ms. Watkins, this is Cal from Advanced Long Distance Movers. We're a couple hours early, so we're already at your building…"

I punch the number back into my phone. The call is picked up on the first ring. "This is Willow Watkins," I say. "I'm about fifteen minutes away."

Looks like my furniture is here, which means my car should be here as well. I checked out of the hotel, knowing the movers were scheduled to arrive this afternoon. I look over the empty conference room to the two large suitcases of the things I'd packed for my first week in Star Falls.

A new deal in the works. A hot new hookup. And a new home. I can never get enough of the excitement for new, new, new. I have a huge grin on my face and an unstoppable feeling in my chest as I grab my roller bags and secure my messenger bag over my shoulder.

The adventure of the next year starts now.

By the time the movers had unloaded my furniture, I'd already corrected a small parking snafu with the condo's management office. Turned out they hadn't secured paid parking with my long-term rental, but a few firm smiles and well-placed calls from my assistant back in Chicago sorted that out.

It's nearly six by the time the movers clear out. My new condo is on the top floor of a luxury building with a view overlooking the river. After yesterday's storm, the sky is still gray, angry clouds drifting past like lazy kittens stretching and rolling across the horizon. The river has a running path, and as twilight settles over Star Falls, I can see strollers and joggers, couples and dogs, filling up the blacktop path.

I look over the boxes and plastic-wrapped furniture with excitement. Setting up a new place and settling into a new home never fails to excite me. I'll be busy all week with site inspections and meeting the contractors we've hired for the renovation of the soon-to-be hottest family eatery in Star Falls. But I'll spend the majority of the week unpacking, finding just the right shelves for my mug collection, the perfect way to display my copper pots and spices. I practically live in the kitchen, and this condo's open floorplan with a massive island was what sold me on making this my home for the next twelve months.

I'm still wearing the pencil skirt and tailored blouse I wore to this morning's SBA meeting, but my feet are bare, and my hair has long fallen loose from the tight bun I'd worn for the presentation.

I'm debating ordering a pizza, changing into sweats, putting on some music, and going deep into unpacking mode, when I'm hit by a sudden craving for kale ravioli.

I bite my lower lip and grab my phone. Jessa answers on the first ring.

"Please tell me you're calling to tell me all about your hot hookup." Her voice sounds shaky, like she's been crying.

"Hey, hey," I say, tempted to switch to video so I can see her. My heart tightens in my chest, and my worries kick into overdrive. "Jess, are you crying? Am I calling at a bad time?"

Her laughter is sad, not bitter, but not funny either. "I'm not even a mom yet, and all I do is worry about keeping this baby safe," she says. "I'm a wreck today. Some days, I'm happy to binge an entire season of *Gossip Girl* while I still can uninterrupted and with a lap full of snacks…"

"Like a lady," I interject.

"Like a damn lady," she corrects, her sniffles louder now. "Okay, I know you called me, but Willow, can we video for a sec?"

I lean against the white marble countertop and prop my phone against a small box labeled "Flatware."

"Jess, I'm here for you, babe. Do it."

I hear static on Jess's end, and she does what I was hoping to. She initiates the video call, and I practically squeal when her beautiful, puffy face comes into frame.

"Oh my God. Look at you. Your new place." Jess wipes her face, and I can see her looking around at my new surroundings.

I shake my head. "Eyes on me, bitch. Tell me who made you cry so I know whose balls I need to squeeze. Or ovaries. I'm an equal opportunity vigilante. Tell me who made you cry."

She shakes her head and points at her belly. "Balls it

is, then. This baby boy… I'm just worried, Willow. Today, I felt some things, and I just spiraled."

I nod and listen to Jessa describe the twinges and pains, the aches and waves of nausea and heartburn that she's been dealing with throughout the time she's been on bed rest. I know as well as she does that the condition she has is serious. This will possibly be the only pregnancy she carries herself. But the doctors have told her she'll have plenty of notice before something goes wrong. She'll have time to get to the hospital. She just needs to rest.

"But how the hell am I supposed to rest when all I want to do is cry?" Her tears flood her face again, and I am hit with an unfamiliar pang of guilt. I wish I could hug her. Wish I could be there to wash her face and bring her tea. To sit beside her as she watches *Gossip Girl* and log her farts and everything, it seems, are important signs that her body is working and the baby is still okay.

A tear slips down my cheek. "I know, Jess. I wish I were there."

That seems to sober her up. She shakes her head and wipes her face with one hand. "Fuck that," she says. "You're living the dream. Now I want to hear everything. Especially about your hookup last night."

I peek at the time on my phone. Jess and I have been talking for a half hour already. I know her mother is staying with her while she's on bed rest, but Jess is single. She decided when she turned forty that she wasn't going to wait around for the right man to have a family. I'm two years older than Jess and filled her ears with reasons why I won't ever have kids and what I truly think men are good for—moving heavy things and giving better orgasms than the vast collection of toys I have. But in the end, Jess decided to go through sperm donation. She knew it would be a tough road, but this tough, this way? Nope.

I ignore the growling of my stomach and decide kale ravioli and chatting with Maggie at Benito's will have to wait until another night. I may not be in hugging reach of Jess, but what I have to give her is what makes our friendship tighter than sisters. Tighter than friends. I have time.

"All right," I tell her totally unironically, flicking on the lights as the sun sets over Star Falls. "But before I tell you about the guy, I have to tell you about the ravioli."

CHAPTER 5
BENITO

"BENITO. Benito. Some delivery guy is up front for you, honey. He says he needs to talk to you?"

My heart freezes in my chest. I'm plating a delicate dish, three spinach and ricotta-stuffed rotolo on a bed of marinara, when my hostess Rita's voice echoes through the kitchen.

"Want me to take it?" Mags's voice is like ice. I can hear the f-bomb she is holding back.

She knows as well as I do there should be no deliveries made from the front of the house, and certainly not at this hour of the day.

She probably expects it's someone making a personal call to demand I get current on a bill or something. Hell, that's what I'm afraid of too.

In my mind, I race through the bills and emails and calls I haven't answered, trying to calculate who might be out front looking for me, but I don't have a damn clue. No matter what it is, I sure as shit can't let Mags handle it.

All day, she's been avoiding me, giving one-word answers to questions and very obviously stepping as far away from me as possible in the cramped kitchen as we work through the dinner rush. She gave the peanut butter crisps I brought from Chloe's to Jasmine, so I know she's *pissed* at me for missing the small business association meeting today. I didn't even try to explain why.

If whatever is going on with Pops is serious—and I can't fucking let my head go there—I'll have to share it eventually. Maybe. Probably. Fuck. One worry at a time.

I plate the rotolo and eyeball Mags. "Take over here?" I ask, wiping my hands on a towel.

She nods but doesn't say anything, stepping into the practiced rhythm of working alongside me. She plates the rest of the dish while I walk through the restaurant toward the front entrance. I have to stop and shake a few hands and clap a few shoulders of the diners who call to greet me, so it takes about ten minutes before I actually make it to the front.

It's well after seven, but the lobby is still full of families waiting for tables to free up for dinner. I don't see anyone who looks official or who looks like they are looking for me, so I step beside Rita behind the hostess desk.

"Sweetheart!" she shouts over the low chatter of my waiting customers. "Benny's here."

I lift my head and follow her hand, which is waving at a fidgety kid who's staring out over the parking lot. He's wearing a blue windbreaker, and his hands are jammed into his pockets.

I squint at him as he approaches, immediately relieved. He is one of the kids I hired over the summer while he was on break from college. If I remember right, I didn't offer Nico a part-time job when school started back up because he was nice enough but a little slow. I feel like I remember a few too many messed-up orders and forgotten side dishes. Mags was the one to tell him we only needed full-time help, essentially letting him go for me. She's always there to take the hard jobs off my hands. The thought of it stresses me out now, but whatever Nico wants, this is something I have to handle alone.

Rita said he had a delivery for me, but maybe that was just a ruse? A way to lure me out front to talk. There's no way this college student is a bill collector now. At least, I sincerely fucking hope not. "Nico? Is that you?"

Nico breaks into a grin and gives me a wave. "Hey, man. Great to see you. Great to be back in the old place." He sniffs the air. "Smells amazing, as usual. You been good?"

I feel my blood start to boil, but I calm my anxiety. This is fine. Everything is fine. "Yeah, man," I say. "Busy as usual." I motion back toward the dining room full of guests. "Dinner rush, you know how it is," I say, trying not to sound like a dick. "Rita said you had a delivery for me?"

The kid's face brightens, and he says, "Yeah. I'm working for Gloria's Floral Fantasies now." At the name of the florist, I hold up a hand. I know the place. That's where I ordered Willow's flowers from this morning. A sinking feeling hits my gut as I wonder what the fuck could have happened. "Let's talk outside." The last thing I want is everyone in my restaurant hearing my private business.

We step out front, and I cock a brow at Nico. "So, you're delivering flowers now?"

He grins. "Yeah, man. It's part time, and it's very cool. I make my own hours, as long as I get the deliveries done within the business day. I can work around my class schedule. It's pretty sweet, actually."

"Good for you." I hear myself saying it, but my foot starts nervously tapping against the pavement. "I hate to rush you, Nic, but I've got to get back to the kitchen."

"Right." Nico slaps his face with a hand and then holds a finger up to me. "One sec, man."

He jogs off toward a large panel van painted with Gloria's distinctive logo on the side in purple. He comes back about a minute later with a beautiful bouquet wrapped in clear cellophane.

"What's this?" I ask, squinting at the bouquet. "Somebody send me flowers?"

Nico chuckles. "Nah, but that'd be sweet, huh?" He holds the bouquet out to me. "You ordered these earlier? The person you sent them to had checked out of the hotel by the time I got there. When I saw the name on the receipt, I figured I'd drop them off here. Or, if you know where the person went, I can try to deliver it there. It's not really protocol. But you know, I worked for you and you're such a great guy, I thought…"

My mind is spinning. These are the flowers I bought for Willow. She's gone? Checked out of the hotel already? A stinging sensation travels through my belly. She's gone. She never even told me her last name.

"Wait," I say. "Did the hotel have any forwarding information for her? Can you try to redeliver if they have an address?"

Nico shakes his head. "Sorry, man. I asked, but they said they don't release that stuff. Privacy and all." He shrugs. "You want me to take the flowers back? You can always call Gloria and ask for a refund. She doesn't normally do that, but seeing as it's you, maybe…"

"Nah." I take the flowers from him and squint through the cellophane. I'm honestly kind of shocked how surprised I am. Deep down, I'd been hoping that by sending my number to Willow, she'd reach out. Want to see me again. My body immediately goes back to last night. To her hotel room. The hot shower, my clammy clothes. Her luscious body tucked beneath mine.

I shake my head to clear the memories. "Look, man," I say. "I've got to get back, and I don't have any cash on me, or I'd tip you. You want to come in for a minute so I can hit the petty cash? Or you can come back with your girlfriend some night for dinner. On the house."

Nico gives me a huge grin. "Free date night? That'd be awesome, Benito. I'll totally take you up on that. Thank you." He claps me on the arm and turns to head back to the van.

I stare down at the massive bundle of flowers in my arms. I see the little plastic fork thing that should hold the card with my message to Willow and my number on it. There's nothing there.

"Nic!" I shout after him. I point to the plastic-covered flowers. "There was supposed to be a card. You got any idea where it is?"

Nico shrugs. "Sorry, man. Must have fallen out. This is my last delivery of the day, so if it's not there, I don't know where it went."

I nod and head back into the restaurant. I'm needed in the kitchen, and I need a way to explain why I've got an armful of white, pink, and red flowers delivered to the front door of my restaurant.

Something deep in my gut twists as I think about Willow. She did say she was new in town, but she didn't say she was staying. I shake my head slowly, rushing back through the restaurant and ducking into my office. I set the bouquet on my desk, completely pissed at myself.

"It was just a hookup," I remind myself. Like dozens of others I've had. No reason to feel disappointed. This is just one hookup that I didn't have to end first. I'm not usually on the receiving end of a diss like this, and I don't love the feeling. But is it really a rejection? How would she even know that I'd follow up? She probably assumed she was just another random hookup. A one-and-done good time.

That's what she is, so whatever this is I'm feeling is just stress from other shit getting under my skin. It has nothing to do with the woman herself.

But even as I'm thinking it, I know I'm lying to myself. Willow was gorgeous. Easy to talk to. Not the first woman who's loved my kale, but... I don't know. I'm, like, deeply pissed that she didn't get my message.

Pissed she'll never know I tried to find her after our one amazing night together.

I sigh and think about what to do with the flowers. I originally thought about getting flowers for Mags, and she *is* really mad. They won't go to waste, and maybe the gesture will earn me a little goodwill with her. God knows the peanut butter crisps weren't enough. She couldn't even be bothered to eat them.

I pick up the house phone and dial the kitchen. Mags answers.

"Hey, can you come back to my office for a sec?" I ask.

"Benito." She sounds pissed, and she should be. It's still the dinner rush.

"Mags, for fuck's sake. Give me five minutes. Please?"

She sighs deep and hard, like an exasperated older sister and not my restaurant's right hand. "On my way," she says, then hangs up without a word.

I grab my cell phone to check my messages while I wait for Mags. I only have one, and it's the one I'm hoping for.

Mom: Benito, it's your mother.

I chuckle to myself. My parents know how texting works, yet they can't manage to stop themselves from identifying who they are in voice mails, emails, and texts. I read on.

Mom: Your father is home, but he won't say anything. He's acting funny. Let's talk when you can. Love you, son. Thank you for letting me lean on you today. You're my heart, Benny. My sweet littlest boy and such a good, good man. Love, Ma

It's a lot to read, and I can hardly process the parts of it. Ma loves all four of us. Franco, Grace, Vito, and then me. But she's always had a special bond with me. Her last baby. Her youngest son.

It's nothing I don't know deep in my soul, but seeing it written out like that, in an awkwardly formal text that's so like Ma, brings a burn of worry and love for my family to my eyes.

I'm blinking fast when my door flies open, and Mags stands in the doorway, arms crossed.

I hold up my hands in surrender. "Come in and shut the door a sec?"

She motions toward the kitchen. "Benny, we're fucking swamped—"

"I know. This'll only take a sec." I nod at the flowers. "I'm sorry I let you down today. Some shit came up, but I want you to know I appreciate you. And I really respect what you do to keep this place—and me—in line."

She squints at the flowers, her face immediately softening. "Wait. This shit's for me? You got me flowers?"

I swallow hard, feeling just the tiniest bit shitty that I didn't actually buy these for Mags. I try telling myself that it's what I had intended to do, that my heart was in the right place, but Mags is already pulling off the clear plastic wrap and sticking her face deep in the blossoms.

"Oh my God," she whispers, drawing in huge breaths from the roses, gardenias, and greens. "These smell amazing. I didn't expect this from you. Fuck, Benito."

She reaches down to pull the empty plastic fork from the center of the bouquet. The flowers are planted in a really pretty white dish, and there must be some kind of foam thing at the bottom, because the plastic fork takes a little work to get out. She tosses that in the trash bin beside my desk and uses both hands to peel back the plastic wrap that protects the whole bouquet.

"I seriously was pissed," she says as she unwraps the flowers. "You know how important that grant is to this place, and you knew how much that meeting meant to me…"

She trails off and I nod, slipping my phone back into the pocket of my jeans. "You can leave those in here until we close," I say, getting up from my desk. "I just wanted you to know I'm sorry I let you down and I appreciate you."

I head past Mags, making my way toward the closed door to get back to the kitchen, when I hear Mags suck in a breath.

"Are you fucking kidding me?"

I turn on my heel and stare. "What?" I ask. "What's the matter?"

Mags is holding a tiny white envelope and a standard florist card between her fingers. Right then and there, my stomach plummets into my toes.

"These flowers were for me, Benito?" She gestures accusingly with the little white card. *"Not as good as the ravioli, but… Thinking of you. B."* She reads the message I'd intended for Willow in a mocking voice. "Nice, Benito. Fucking classy. I'm sorry if this comes off as disrespect, because no matter what, it's your name out front. This is your place and all that shit. But this?" She drops the flowers on my desk so hard, I'm shocked the planter dish doesn't shatter. "You really can be a major dick sometimes."

She throws the white card on the floor and storms past me. Then she marches out of my office and slams the door in my face.

Shame floods my cheeks, and I head back to my desk to drop into my chair. The dinner rush is not going to wind down anytime soon, but something tells me I'll be managing the kitchen on my own the rest of the night.

And despite my best intentions, like everything else in my life lately, I can't help but feel I'm getting exactly what I deserve.

I haven't said much other than what was required since I came back to the kitchen. After the last customer clears out, I send the kitchen staff home. I want to be alone in my kitchen, and I can't stand the silent questioning, the accusing looks. I can't stand having all the ways I suck at everything being rubbed in my face by the people I'm supposed to lead.

My employees. My kitchen. My team.

After the bussers have the floor done and prepped, a couple of the servers pop in to say goodnight, looking like they want to try to figure out what happened between Mags and me tonight by reading it off the kitchen walls or something.

But I stay silent, angry at myself. Angry at Nico for not delivering the flowers before Willow checked out. Angry at my dad for making my mom worry. I'm just fucking angry, and I'm taking my feelings out on a dirty stockpot and a scouring sponge when one of my mom's best friends, Sassy, fake knocks on the kitchen door.

"Hey there, boss." She cocks a painted-on brow at me and unties her apron. She yawns and checks the time. "It's awfully late to find you here rage-cleaning. You want to talk about it?"

The look I give her must answer for me because Sassy crosses her thick arms over her generous chest. "Well, all right, then," she says, sounding put out. "You want to sulk about whatever shit you pulled on Mags tonight, that's your business."

She turns to leave as if the threat of her leaving will convince me to change my mind, but I don't say shit. I turn the hot water tap hotter and scour until I think I'll rub a hole in the stainless steel.

Sassy hesitates, and then I know I'm in trouble. My mother's close-knit friends treat me like family, but tonight, I'm not in the mood. I'm just not interested in sharing all the ways I've fucked up with Sassy. Not tonight.

"Benito," she starts, but I stiffen and don't look up. She knows me well enough to know that when I go silent, it takes an act of God or threats from my ma to get me talking. She sighs softly. "Get some rest, sweetheart. See you tomorrow." Her voice is gentle, a lot less probing, and I hear the care buried under the sass.

I wait until I hear the solid clack of her sturdy shoes

before I go back to scrubbing as though I could clean the shit feelings away if I just worked the pot hard enough.

A second later, another voice breaks me from washing. And I'm just about to lose my shit when I see it's Rita.

"Benito?" she calls. "You in here, honey?"

I drop the scouring pad in resignation. "By the sinks, Rita." My voice is flat, and I know I sound like a damn child. But I can't help it. I just want five minutes alone with my thoughts in my kitchen. Alone with my failures and fuckups. I'm still responsible for this place, no matter how out of control I feel. It should be fucking obvious that I need to be left alone. But for Rita, I pull back my temper and draw in a breath.

Rita walks up to me, and I feel her small hand on my back. "Honey, could I ask a favor?"

I crane my neck to look back at her. I'm immediately concerned that something's up with her. Rita never asks me for anything. Hell, she didn't even want me walking her to the car last night in a torrential downpour.

"What do you need?" I ask, turning off the faucet and giving her my full attention.

She motions toward me with both hands, gesturing for me to bend down. Puzzled, I do what I think she wants. She takes my face in her hands the same way my ma does. She closes her eyes and squeezes my face lightly in her veined, knobby hands.

She draws in a deep breath and then sighs. "Benito, I'm not your mother. But if Lucia were here, she'd want someone to be honest with you." She presses her neon-pink lips together—a bold and dramatic shade for a woman of any age. "Take a goddamn day off, would you? You look like you're about to blow. Go for a run, go get laid. Whatever you young people do these days. Play some of those violent video games I hear so much about." She frees my face and nods. "I'm worried about you. And a lot of other people are too. Even if we don't all know how to show it."

I scrub a wet hand across my eyebrows, the tenderness and her lack of prying freeing me up a little. "I…I fucked up, Rita," I admit quietly. "With Mags. With a lot of things."

She shrugs, pushing heavily bejeweled glasses onto her forehead. "Who doesn't? So what?" She taps her chest. "We all know your heart, Benito. Say you're sorry and get back to doing what you do so well."

What is that? I wonder. I'm not sure I even know anymore.

Instead, I say, "We need a new fucking roof before winter, Rita. You got a rich boyfriend we could hit up for some cash?"

She barks a laugh. "Baby, I'm good. But I'm not *that* good."

I wink at her. "You'd school me, Rita. You'd teach me things a man could only dream of."

She shakes her head and points a neon-pink nail at me. She must paint her nails every day to match her lipstick. "If I were thirty years younger, Benito…"

"Thirty!" I exclaim. "Rita, I'm thirty-one. You'd still be, what? Fortysomething?"

"Fortysomething," she confirms coyly, not willing to

reveal her real age, even though she knows I've got that information on her employment paperwork. "Nothing wrong with a little age gap."

I wave her away. "Goodnight, Rita. Samuel picking you up?"

She nods and blows me a kiss. "I locked the front doors. I'll go out the employee entrance."

I dry my hands and pat my pocket for my keys. "It's dark out back. I'll let you out the front." I walk her out the front, waving a hand at Samuel, who's idling in the lot with his brights on. Then I lock up and head to the kitchen.

I take a long, deep breath. I'm finally alone. The restaurant is quiet. Even the heat has turned off due to the automatic timers Mags set up last year.

She said we'd save a shit-ton on utilities with the smart controls set to heat and cool on a schedule, and of course, as always, she was right. But that means not even the old furnace is knocking as I get back to work. It's peaceful, being here alone. The place I've built at thirty-one years old. My dreams, my sweat. Even my tears.

After a little more listless scrubbing, I finally give the old stockpot a break. It's nearly ten before I head into my office, throw the card Mags tossed onto the floor into the trash, grab the damn flowers, and head out to my SUV.

I make the drive home, thinking about how the hell I'm going to apologize to Mags. Maybe I can reach out to the SBA and ask for a meeting. See what I missed in the presentation about the community development grant thing that Mags wants me to apply for. Maybe I should call out sick for a couple days. As long as Mags is there, the kitchen will run fine. I spend every waking minute there. It might do everybody some good if I took the damn break everyone seems to think I need. I don't know. If I stay home, I'll check my email. I'll worry. No, fuck that. I'll obsess. Over the roof, the bills, the paperwork.

I love being in the kitchen. I love cooking. Maybe I could take a day off and test out some new recipes at home. Call up my pops and see if he wants to head into Cleveland for a trip to the specialty markets. Pops. I didn't reply to my mom's text earlier, so that's something I can do if I take a day off. Go visit my parents. See if I can get to the bottom of what's up with Mario and Lucia.

I pull into my assigned underground parking space and juggle the flowers in my arms. I ride the elevator to the top floor of the building before I realize that I don't want these damn things. I should have known the card would have fallen someplace inside the plastic. I wasn't thinking. I shouldn't have tried to regift them to Mags. So many should haves and shouldn'ts.

When the door opens on my floor, I don't even head toward my unit. I turn the opposite way and head for the utility closet where the trash chute is located. I'm going to chuck this entire bouquet down the chute and put this whole damn day behind me.

I yank open the utility closet door, but the light is on and someone's in there, struggling to open the trash chute and fit a very full bag of trash inside.

"Hey, uh, you need a hand?" I ask. I know almost

everyone in this building, but I don't recognize the woman in front of me.

She turns at the sound of my voice and says, "Thanks, I just moved in. Is there some trick to keeping this thing open while you put your trash…"

Her words die on her lips as we blink at each other in shock.

The woman throwing her trash out in my building is none other than my hot hookup from last night. The woman standing in front of me in black yoga pants, a loose top that's falling over one shoulder, and a messy bun is Willow.

CHAPTER 6
WILLOW

I LEAN FORWARD and stroke the rich, velvety petals of a dark red rose. "You did *not*," I gasp. "Please tell me you did not regift flowers from one woman to another."

Ben leans across my white marble counter and grabs the bouquet. "This little fucker has caused me more trouble…"

"I blame the man," I say playfully, yanking the bouquet out of his hands and setting it protectively by the sink. "Not the flowers. And since these were meant for me, I think I'll keep them, thank you very much. They've come full circle. Finally made it home."

Something about saying that, finally coming home, sends a cold shiver skating down my spine, and the hairs on my arms lift in warning. *Homes are temporary*, I remind myself. Everything is temporary. These cut flowers won't last more than a couple days, maybe a week, if I water and feed them. Nothing is meant to stay in one place forever. Not people, not flowers.

I turn back to Ben, who is unwrapping thick moving paper from my barstools. They are really heavy, and the movers offered to unwrap them. But by the time everything else was inside, the bed set up, and most of the furniture reassembled, I didn't have the energy to have strangers spend another minute in my place. I'll gladly accept a little help from Ben though.

"While you literally find yourself a chair," I say, opening my completely empty fridge, "can I offer you some tap water? You might have to drink it from your hand, though. I haven't unpacked the glasses yet."

Ben crinkles up a load of brown moving paper and sets a vintage bronze barstool in front of the kitchen island. "Here okay?"

I nod. "Perfect. Although now that you saved my behind in the trash room, you're going to have to show me where to recycle all my moving boxes and the packing paper."

A slow grin spreads over his face. "Should we also toss out the evidence that you cheated on the best restaurant in Star Falls by ordering from—" he squints at a small pizza box resting on the counter near the flowers "—Papa Gino's pizza? A chain, Willow? How could you order mass-produced pizza when you claimed just last night that food is your life?"

"Food *is* my life," I insist. "But there are times when cheap food is nostalgic. Some of my best memories were made over a gas station taquito or hot dog."

"And some of your worst memories probably happened after eating that crap too." He's smirking, but I'm not going to join in on the joke.

The memories of road trips with friends, of the many things I've chosen to do in my adulthood with people who choose to spend their time with me, are running through my memory. Maybe he's always lived in Star Falls and had gourmet meals. I sure as hell didn't. But I don't want my issues to ruin what might otherwise turn into a really fun night.

I arch a brow and come around the island to lean against the cool marble beside him. "So," I say, looking him over. "I'm not exactly great at math, but I put two and two together. You're Benito, king of Italian cuisine. Am I right?"

He sucks his lower lip into his mouth like he's biting back a laugh. "Well, I am Benito Bianchi," he confirms, stretching out a hand to me. "Creator of Italian delicacies, regifter of flowers, and savior of ladies who can't figure out trash chutes."

I take his hand and hold it in mine, and almost without meaning to, I trace my fingers across the back of his knuckles. His hands are strong and warm, the kind of hands that could shape dough or tug my hair with equal intensity. I know because I've already experienced one of those. Despite what seems like a giant ego on this man, I can't say that I'd mind experiencing him again.

As I stroke his hand with my fingers, the air between us sizzles with the memories of last night. The unspoken question of whether we're headed in that direction again sparks between us like fireflies on a summer night, suddenly playful and unexpected.

Hooking up with Ben might be more complicated

now. I know a little about who he is. I know about his business, his roof, his kitchen manager, and her none-too-subtle frustration at Benito's business practices. As if that wasn't enough, we're next-door neighbors. For a woman who never likes to dig too deep or stay too long, this situation already feels like far too much.

"Do you prefer Ben?" I ask, switching the topic to something neutral. "Or was that just your bar name? You know, the one you give hookups if you want to stay anonymous."

He chuckles. "I'm never anonymous. Not in a town like Star Falls."

I resist the urge to roll my eyes, because he doesn't even sound like he's boasting. In a town this small and quaint, I'm sure it's true.

When he turns to face me, his stare is intense. I feel like I'm under a spotlight, and yet, it's not uncomfortable.

I feel my body come awake under his gaze, like my limbs are flowers starving for the kind of light only he can produce. I no longer feel the sore feet and tired hands from moving and standing all day.

What are the odds that Ben would have tried to send me flowers? That we'd end up being neighbors?

Despite all the reasons why I should thank him for the tour of the trash room and send him home, my resolve to stay professional and keep my distance from this confusing and charismatic man crumples with just one flick of his tongue across his plump lower lip.

"My family calls me Benny," he says, his voice rumbling with something that sounds like pride. "Benito when my ma's mad. I answer to just about anything, but I'd really prefer if you called me something more descriptive."

I can't even stop myself. The flirtation comes out of me, despite whatever warnings my logical brain is trying to send to stop this. "What would you like me to call you?" I ask. "Sex god? Ravioli-making rake? Deliveryman of dinner and orgasms?"

He grins. "I resemble those remarks."

I lace my fingers through his. "You do. You were sexy in a freezing rainstorm, Benny," I say, trying out the cute version of his name. "I think you should be very, very flattered. I meant those things as a compliment."

He turns quickly and slides a hand under my hair, his fingers brushing the tender skin of my neck. "I am flattered," he says, bending low and whispering hot against my ear. "And excited. I thought I'd never see you again."

"And here *we* are." My eyes flutter shut, and I breathe him in deep. On the surface, I pick up notes of garlic and olive oil. But deeper, I smell a hint of cologne and mint, and another hot, delicious scent that my body immediately remembers from last night. From when he was naked, his limbs thrown over mine, his bare skin smooth and hot beneath me and around me.

"So," I rasp, my voice thick in my throat, "aren't you going to ask me my last name? You might decide you want to have flowers delivered again in the future."

He lowers his lips to my ear and kisses my earlobe, his fingers still firm behind my neck. "Nah," he murmurs, snaking his fingers through the hair at the base of my loose bun. "I'll make sure all my deliveries are made in person from here on out. More personal that way. I wouldn't want the card to get lost and have you think that Papa Gino was trying to get in your pants."

I chuckle and give in to whatever this is. Benito is a man of contradictions. He's a little cocky, but I kind of prefer him hot and full of himself, actually.

It's easier to focus on his body and the obvious chemistry we share than to think about the man himself. His business. His staff. His heart. This is just about the connection, and connections can be light and easy.

"I like the sound of you getting in my pants, Benito." I turn my face toward his, my eyes still closed. The heat of him warms me from my fingertips to my bare toes, and the slight tug of his fingers in my hair sends a tremor through my body. A low moan slips from my lips.

"Willow." He says my name like it's his favorite food. I can feel his lips shape every letter as he speaks. "I want to put you on this counter and have my way with your pussy. But I don't think the marble is going to feel as good for you as I want it to."

Another shiver claims my flesh, and I feel my knees buckle slightly. "My bed is unpacked," I say, the words slow, my limbs drowsy with arousal. I lean forward, pressing myself against his hips, and feel the erection straining against the front of his jeans. "But I have no idea where the condoms are in this mess."

"My place?" he asks. "I'll drive."

I pull my face back and grin at him. "I have a car now, you know. No more rideshares."

He scoops me up in his arms, and I wrap my legs around his waist. "I'll insist on giving you a ride. Where are your house keys?"

I point to a lanyard inside a small brushed-bronze bowl on a sideboard near the front door. "You don't think it will be awkward carrying me over the threshold of your place? It might give the neighbors the wrong impression."

His mouth is on mine, crushing my lips, his strong hands cupping my ass as he stumbles toward my front door with my legs still wrapped tight around his hips. "Fuck the neighbors," he rasps, staggering across the condo until he's pressing my ass against my door.

He pulls his lips from mine, and I gasp. "I'm a neighbor now, so, yes, please."

"Keys," he barks. I reach for the bowl and grab my keys, clutching them in one hand. Then he leans into me, and my vision goes dark as he kisses me until I can't breathe.

When we're both gasping for air, he sets me gently on my feet, yanks open my door, then grabs my hand.

I walk the twenty or so steps down the hallway carpet in my bare feet and watch while Benny digs into his pocket for a set of keys. He curses quietly to himself as his trembling hands fumble with the lock. When the door finally swings open, he reaches for me and tugs me inside. I realize I haven't even stopped for my phone. I'm going inside the place of a guy I hardly know. My new neighbor. I don't have a way to call or text, no alarm to set if we fall asleep like we did last night.

I don't know what's come over me, but I don't care.

Benny flips on a light, and a warm yellow glow brings his place to life. I feel oddly safe here, comfortable. Like I can already see a future spending a lot of time going between his place and mine.

He's not a serial killer, I tell myself. Serial killers don't bring women home to their place when they live next door. Serial killers don't send women flowers after a one-night stand. Serial killers don't make gorgeous ravioli and own businesses in small towns.

"Willow?" My name on his lips has me looking up at him. He's watching me, the deep brown stare intense. His cheeks are flushed, a light stubble on his face revealing the tiny cleft at the tip of his chin that I remember from last night.

He's backlit by the soft glow of a large light fixture that hangs over his island. The marble is different, the place much more lived-in than mine, of course. But it's warm and masculine. His kitchen is dark, the marble a sleek black sparkling with swirls of gold. I feel oddly happy to be here, and something deep inside wants to name it. Wants to think about why, but I won't go there. Not tonight.

"I was promised some personal attention," I remind him.

He growls, an animalistic sound, and his eyes flutter shut for a moment. "Come on." He takes my hand and leads me to the room that must be his bedroom. His unit is actually bigger than mine. He has two bedrooms, and I'm assuming another partially open door leads to a second bath.

Suddenly, the rush of getting to his place slows

down. Something about going into his bedroom… This feels different from a sexy, anonymous hookup in a hotel. This is his home. Where he sleeps. Where people he's dated have stayed.

I look over the dark room while he turns on a small bedside light using an app on his phone. The curtains on the window are open, and the moonlight that's reflected off the river outside casts a white glow over the room.

"Willow." His voice is quiet.

I step into his arms and lift my face. He kisses me lightly, probingly, as if he's tasting a brand-new dish for the first time. His lips are light on mine as he presses and licks, explores my tongue and the depths of my open mouth. His breath is so natural, so sweet. It's like our bodies perfectly balance each other. I close my eyes and reach for his ass, pulling our hips close.

"Willow," he says again.

I hum my response against his lips.

"I do want to know your last name," he whispers. "I don't want to have to stalk your discarded junk mail to figure it out."

I giggle and pull my face back from his. "Watkins," I say. "Willow Watkins. Nice to meet you."

"It's so fucking good to meet you," he says, wrapping his hands around my hips and picking me up again.

He sets me down on the edge of his bed. It's made, but hardly. The white down comforter has been tossed across the king-sized mattress but not really smoothed, and I can see the edge of his dark-green sheets because he hasn't bothered to cover the entire surface of the massive bed. His pillows are all wonky, like he rolled out of bed after clutching them in his arms and bunching them under his head and they've patiently been waiting there in the same position for his return. I can understand the feeling.

When he leans me back against the soft covers, I look up at the ceiling and lift my hips, letting him strip off my yoga pants. The cool air meets my bare flesh and raises goose bumps on my thighs, but I'm not moving. Not covering up. I feel exposed but not vulnerable. Sharing pleasure, showing him my body… That's easy. And I love it when relationships are easy.

Benny kneels next to the bed, and he's pulling off my panties and setting them someplace out of my sight. I flutter my eyes closed and give in to the feeling of his warm palms skating up the length of my thighs. I moan, a soft but greedy sound. He's just barely touching my skin, but already, I am starving for more of him.

He tugs gently at my hips, urging me toward the end of the bed so he can kneel on the floor and reach my pussy with his mouth. I feel kisses following his fingers, first along the tops of my thighs and then between my legs and along my inner thighs.

His breathing is ragged against my skin, and my nipples tighten deliciously, a thrill radiating from my breasts, through my belly, until the pulse pounds in my core.

He widens my legs, pressing my knees open. "Willow," he gasps, "you smell like fucking cherry syrup. Sweet and…" I feel his lips against my seam, and my hips buck. "I'm not going to be able to hold back," he mutters, turning his head and cursing against the tender skin of my thigh. "You got to talk to me, babe," he says. "Smack me in the back of the head if you have to. I don't want to do too much, but fuck, you're beautiful."

I reach down and slide my fingers through his thick, soft hair. The waves of it are smooth, like he doesn't even use styling product, and the heat from his skin radiates into my tightening grasp. "You won't be too much," I tell him. "But I might be too much for you. I know what I need to come," I warn him.

"Take it," he begs. "Take it from me, babe. Don't hold anything back from me."

His words do something funny to me. He sounds sincere. This isn't just dirty talk he's trying on to see what it does to me. He doesn't sound like he's trying to impress me now, the cocky bravado totally replaced by intensity.

When he lowers his mouth to my pussy and I feel the lightest touch of a fingertip, I gasp, and he praises me.

"Yeah, baby. Help me learn what you like. You like this?" He strokes me in long, smooth touches, the pressure so delicate, I want to thrust my hips against him to speed him up.

"Fuck, yes." Part of me wants to pull back a little. Communicating like this is rare for me.

I force my body to relax, my legs to open. I try hard to get the hell out of my head and let him lead our pace. This is different from last night. More intimate, if that's possible. It feels good but also scary.

"Is there anything you don't like?" he murmurs, and I feel the light rasp of his breath on my trimmed hairs.

His hands don't stop kneading me. It's like his palms are massaging me while his fingers stroke me. I can't keep track of everything I feel, but it's all so, so good.

I'm lost in a haze of bliss and warmth, all of it coming from his voice, his touch.

"I'll tell you," I promise. "You won't break me."

With that, he lowers his lips to my clit and flicks the hot tip of his tongue against me. He slides one finger inside me while he sucks my clit into his mouth.

The pleasure is immediately intense, but perfect. He matches every movement of my hips, every gasp and groan with more pressure, faster movements, or by slowing down agonizingly. I grip the sheets in my hands and lift my knees, propping my feet on his shoulders.

"Fuck, yes, Willow. You're so goddamn perfect. You're beautiful. Fuck," he grates out, lifting his mouth only for a second from my clit. "Fuck my face, babe. Take what you want." As soon as he gets the words out, he goes right back to sucking me while he maintains the slow, relentless strokes of his fingers inside me.

By the time I feel the intensity building, I'm holding his head and rocking my hips hard against his mouth.

"More," I beg him. "Your fingers… Fuck me, Benny. Oh God, fuck me harder."

He pistons two fingers inside me, his mouth keeping a steady pressure on my clit, and even though I can't make out the words, he's muttering, whispering against my pussy, urging me, praising me as I grind and grind.

I lift my hips and work my hands in his hair, chasing the climax that's just out of reach, every nerve ending in my nipples and core liquid and melted, aching and desperate.

With every groan I feel against my flesh, the rumble of his curses, his breaths, his kisses, he adds just the right friction to send me skyward.

When I finally come, it hits me like a blast of wind, pushing, pushing, pushing me through wave after wave of pleasure. The sensation is harder, more intense than any I can remember.

As my body releases, my legs collapse against the bed, and he turns his face to rest his head against my thigh. He's panting, and I'm completely out of breath, the pounding of my heart so fierce in my chest, I'm sure he can hear it.

"I'm so fucking glad I found you," he says.

I pull my weak fingers from his hair, and we just lie there together for what seems like minutes, neither one of us speaking, neither one of us breaking the erotic spell. This feels right. Like I could crawl up the down comforter, tuck myself under, and cuddle into his pillows. As long as his body was spooned right there behind me.

I could imagine never leaving.

Never getting enough of this.

As my body cools and I come down from a place so lust-drenched and delicious, I feel like I can hardly think straight, his words echo in my mind. I hear what he said with stark and sudden clarity.

I'm so fucking glad I found you.

And that's why I jump out of bed, throw on my yoga pants, and run.

CHAPTER 7
BENITO

BETWEEN HAVING a gorgeous woman literally run from my bed to the bullshit I've been dealing with in the kitchen with Mags all week, I practically collapse when I finally make it over to my parents' house.

I arrive at my parents' early, hoping to score a few minutes alone with Ma before the chaos of my three siblings, their spouses, and the many kids. But my hopes are pretty much dashed when my sister Grace opens the door.

"What the hell, shithead," she says, leaning forward to kiss me on the cheek. "You're early."

"What'd I do now?" I ask, kissing her back. Gracie's long black hair is up in a sleek ponytail, and at my question, she lifts a perfectly shaped black brow at me.

"Nothing, Benny. Absolutely nothing. Ryder's parents took the kids to the city for a sleepover for the weekend, so I'm kid-free. I'm cursing and drinking while I've got the chance. As long as Ma doesn't hear me. I have no spare change for the swear jar." She nudges me in the ribs. "For reals. You're never here before the food is on the table. What happened? Restaurant burn down?"

I say a silent prayer and look for some wood to knock. "Don't even joke about that," I tell her. But the fact that Grace is swearing and sassy makes things feel a little more normal. I need some normal today. I need my family today. This is home, and I'm so grateful I have this place to come to.

I flick Gracie in the ribs like she nudged me, but harder, little-brother style.

"Hey!" she yells. "Stop."

"What's the yelling about?" Ma pads into the hallway, her brows furrowed in full mama mode, until she sees me. Her face immediately shifts into a look of concern. "Benito? Baby, what's wrong?"

She practically pushes past Grace to get to me.

"Thanks, Ma," Grace says, plopping down on the couch with my parents' dogs. The little Chihuahua tucks down into Gracie's lap, and Grace swaddles her in a blanket. "I'm just the one who got flicked in the rib cage. I'm totally fine. Don't worry about me."

"You hush," Ma says, nodding severely at Grace. "Let me discipline your brother."

I shake my head. I am thirty-one years old, I own a business, and I haven't lived at home for nearly ten years. But you're never too old to be disciplined by Lucia Bianchi—not if you deserve it.

Ma glares at me as she reaches for my face, and I bend down to kiss her. She grips me tight, pushing up on her bare toes to hug me. "My heart," she whispers in my ear. "Is everything okay?"

"I can hear you," Gracie says, sounding bored. "You want me to leave? You guys need some mother-son privacy? I'll go find Pops and tell him some secrets of my own."

Ma and I look at each other, and I nod at my sister. "Would you?" I ask in a low voice. "I'm not shitting you, Gracie."

Grace gets up off the couch, carrying the Chihuahua bundle in her arms. She stares at me, her heavy wings of eyeliner missing for the more casual family dinner. "What the shit is going on?" she asks.

"Gracie." Ma doesn't even have to get it out. My sister holds up a hand and stops her.

"Sorry, Ma, sorry. Why do I feel like you two really are telling secrets? What's up?" She looks from me to our mother, a sincerely worried look on her face.

"I got into some hot water with Mags." I think fast and then explain. "It's nothing. Ma and I talked about it the other day. I was going to update her."

Grace has a bold personality and takes no shit from anyone. But the one thing my sister has is a seriously generous heart. She juggles Ma's dog in her arms and nods. "You need another ear, you can bend mine. You two talk. I'll go find Pops."

"He's in the basement, Gracie," Ma calls, which cracks me up because unless my pops is in the kitchen, the only other place he'd be before a Sunday dinner is the basement, where we have a whole second kitchen. Smaller, but when you raise four kids under one roof in a modest home, a second kitchen is a necessity, not a luxury.

Once Gracie goes downstairs, I lean close to ask Ma about the latest with Pops. She shakes her head. "He won't say a word, Benny. I asked him what it was all about, why he's so secretive about going to the doctor, but he just said it was routine and not to worry."

I'd ask Ma if she's tried that, but "not worry" and my ma are two things that never have gotten along together. I nod. "Well, sooner or later, you're going to get a doctor's bill or a co-pay statement from your insurance, right? That should have the name of the doctor on it, and then you just ask him. You show him the paperwork, and you demand he give you the news."

Ma looks elated at first and then just as quickly deflates. "I never even thought of that," she says. "You're right. But how can I go all private detective on your father? I don't even want to. Things between us have never been like that, Benito. We've been together since we were fifteen years old. How many secrets do you think we've kept from each other?" She holds up a hand, her fingers circling together to form an O. "Zero. No secrets. We tell each other everything. I want him to tell me what's going on of his own free will. I'm not going to go all Sherlock Holmes on Mario."

I don't blame her. I'd want to know too. I can't imagine why Pops would be holding out on Ma, unless it's serious. "You want me to say something?" I ask. "I'll tell him right now that I know he had a doctor's appointment last week and—"

The sound of Gracie bellowing as she stomps up the basement steps stops me cold.

"So, Pops, you made two pans of lasagna?" She's practically screaming.

I groan and shake my head at Ma. "She needs fucking acting lessons, that one."

Ma grimaces, and I hold up a hand. "Sorry, sorry. Freaking. Freaking acting lessons."

Pops throws open the door, carrying a steaming hot pan of lasagna between two well-worn, red-checkered oven mitts. "Benny," he cries out, looking over his shoulder at my sister. "Gracie, why didn't you say your brother was here?"

She doesn't answer and gives me a death glare, her eyebrows bouncing up and down on her expressive face. "Well, Pops, you're on your way up. I didn't think Benny getting here was exactly front-page news." She sounds grumpy, but her attitude is directed at me.

I step away from Ma, knowing our conversation is finished. She reaches for my arm, though, and gives it a squeeze. "Benito…" she says.

"I got it, Ma. I'll help Pops with the other tray."

I can hear her huff a sigh of relief. She knows I won't confront my pops until she says she's ready. But I'm uncomfortable as I follow Pops into the kitchen. He sets the lasagna down on a dish towel and then turns to hug me.

"Benito." He holds me tight. This isn't just a quick welcome, a routine peck, or a slap on the back. Pops is holding me. "Great to see you, son. I didn't expect you so early. You need to take off right away? You're staying for dinner, aren't you?"

I nod slowly, releasing my dad even more slowly. I try to look him over for signs that something's different. Same thick, graying hair that stands in waves like mine. Same reading glasses Ma forced him to get not that long ago. He even smells the same, the faint whiff of his cologne hitting my nose as I clap him on the back of his flannel shirt.

He gives me a huge smile, then gestures excitedly to the lasagna. "Make a plate, son. I don't want to hold you up. Eat, eat."

I shake my head. "It's all right, Pops. Mags is covering dinner tonight. I'm not going in to work."

That may have been the worst possible thing I could have said. Now my dad's looking at me like I said I wanted to put ketchup on his lasagna. "Mags? Running the kitchen? Benny, what's going on? Is everything okay at the restaurant?"

I nod and wave a hand at him. I don't know what to tell him. Part of me wants to share the shit going on. The roof, the SBA grant that Mags wants me to apply for, the mix-up with the flowers that Mags still hasn't forgiven me for. But then I think about my dad, his heart, his who knows what. How can I stress him out with my shit when I don't know how stress will affect him?

I rub my face and head to the fridge for the pitcher of water. My throat is suddenly dry. I've never, literally never, been in this situation with my parents before. I've hidden shit from them all my life, but nothing serious.

Getting drunk at prom and throwing up on the rented shoes. Crashing Pops's truck the first time I used it alone because my girlfriend at the time was trying to jerk me off while I was behind the wheel. Sneaking a whole unopened bottle of wine to drink in the basement with my brothers on a hot summer night.

All that shit, though… It's kid shit. Normal growing-up stuff. Not secrets. Not like whatever it is Pops is hiding from Ma.

"You make the salad yet?" I ask.

My dad's face breaks into a massive grin. "It's been years since we cooked together. You got the tomatoes?"

I grab a couple of tomatoes and groan. "Pops, you need me to go shopping for you? These look like something the dog shit out."

My dad cackles, but then he comes over to inspect them over my shoulder. "Are they that bad? I just bought them this week. I was up in—" He stops himself suddenly. "Well, if you think they're bad, son, just toss them."

My heart shudders in my chest.

Total lockdown.

He bought these earlier this week when he was in the city. These aren't from the local market. But this is clearly something he doesn't want to talk about.

I debate whether I should press him on the issue, ask him where he got them from, but I let it go. Pops was about to say it, and then he stopped.

Whatever it is he's got going on, he's not ready to share it. And no matter how much it's killing me, I'm not going to push.

At least, not yet.

The four of us are just about to sit down to eat when Vito lets himself into the house.

"Dumbass," Gracie and I both call out at the same time.

My mother scolds us as Vito shakes his head. "You know, that never gets old." He slips off his boots.

Ma gets up from the table to hug him. "Vito," she says, leaving a big maroon smear on his cheek. "Where's my grandbaby? Where's Eden?"

Vito goes right to Pops, leans over his chair, and smooches his cheek loudly, then smacks me on the back in greeting. "Asshole," he mutters warmly. "What the hell you doing here so early?"

The question is actually starting to grate on my nerves. I run a business. I'm sorry I haven't been able to make family dinners for the last ten years. I've slipped out of my own family eatery almost every Sunday to at least sit down with my family for an hour. They're making it sound like an act of God that I'm here and not rushing to get back to Benito's. I guess, in a way, it is, but I'm starting to feel like the asshole they keep saying I am.

I lift my wineglass and ignore my brother's question.

"Franco and Chloe coming?" he asks.

Ma shakes her head. "What do I know? Nobody tells me anything. I still don't know where my grandbaby is."

Vito nods. "Junie's cutting a molar. She's running a

low-grade fever, been napping all afternoon. Eden stayed behind."

Ma immediately starts making suggestions, offering to make soup and things for the little girl Vito shares with his longtime girlfriend, Eden. Juniper's biological dad gave up all parental rights, and Vito and Eden are in the process of both planning a wedding and having Vito legally adopt Juniper as his own.

Vito serves himself some salad, not even noticing that no one else has food on their plates when Ma starts yelling at him as the door opens again. This time, it's Franco, the eldest.

"Yo, yo," Franco says in the way only he can. He yanks off his motorcycle boots and holds up his hands. "Got to wash up. Just helped a lady on the side of the road with a flat tire."

My brother is a mechanic, so it's not surprising he'd help a lady in distress, even on a Sunday. He comes back to the table after he washes up in the powder room and, starting with Ma, gives everyone kisses or hugs hello. "Chloe couldn't make it," he explains, taking the chair next to me. "You're here early," he says, nodding. "Good to see you here, man. You staying?"

I nod. "Where's Chloe?"

Franco points to his nose. "She feels like she's coming down with a cold or something. Doesn't want to spread the germs. You'll have to put up with just me tonight."

I reach for the bottle of Chianti and fill Franco's glass. He looks around the table. "Looks like I'm right on time." He lifts his glass in the air. "The OG Bianchis."

"This is really something." My pops sounds emotional. He lifts up his wineglass. "All my kids together at one time." We all raise our glasses and then drink. "I love the spouses and the partners and the grandkids, but this is special." Dad's quiet for a moment, then he gets up from the table. "I forgot something. Excuse me." He pushes back from his chair and heads into the kitchen.

Gracie and Franco start talking about work, while Vito immediately starts eating his salad.

Ma and I are the only ones who exchange worried looks.

"Should I help him?" I ask the question quietly, hoping only Ma will hear, but Gracie, with her damned bat ears, points across the table at me.

"What the fuck, Benny? What's with all the whispers?"

"Language, Gracie." I say it in my best impersonation of Ma, and both Franco and Vito burst out laughing.

Gracie looks pissed, and Ma's got a deeply worried look on her face, but we all shut up pretty quick when Pops returns. He's holding a brick of cheese and a grater. We're all silent, Gracie glaring at me, Franco and Vito looking at Gracie, and Ma and me eyeballing Pops.

Mario looks over the table, then holds up the brick of cheese, a perfect forest-green wax sealing one side of the triangle. "Parmigiano-Reggiano," Pops says. "Who wants cheese on their lasagna?"

Ma and I visibly relax, while Vito holds up his plate. "Where's the grater I got you for Christmas, Pops?"

My father thinks for a moment, then sets down the flat old-school stainless-steel grater. "Let me find it."

"Nah, forget it. I'm yanking your chain, Pops. Top me off." Vito holds out his plate, and our dad grates a healthy mound of the rich, aged cheese over V's lasagna.

I'm just about to take a bite when I hear the harsh buzzing of somebody's phone.

Everybody starts hollering about whose phone it is, but I can tell from the vibrating tone it's mine. I thought I left my phone in my glove box, but I must have had it in my pocket and set it down near the couch when I said hello to Gracie. I grab it from the coffee table and swipe to silence the alert. I have two texts from Mags, one after the other.

Mags: B, sorry, I know you're taking tonight for family dinner, but this is a 911. How soon can you get here?

And then, just a few minutes later:

Mags: No one's hurt. But this is IMPORTANT.

These messages are more civil than anything Mags has said since I tried to regift Willow's flowers to her.

I rub my forehead and sigh. Fuck. The timing.

I hate having to choose, but Mags said 911. I've got to go.

I head back to my seat and shovel a bite of food into my mouth. "Sorry," I say, holding up my phone. "It's Mags. I got to go in."

Ma wordlessly gets up from the table and grabs my plate. I know she's going to try to send me home with my food, so I stop her. "Ma, I'll eat at the restaurant. Save those for me, though. I'll stop this week for lunch."

I blow a kiss to my pops, who waves at me while he listens to Vito telling him about Eden's new job. She started working for Gracie's husband's business and seems to be thriving there. Pops is engrossed, so I take an extra minute to look back over the table before I leave.

Ma is passing Vito more salad. Franco and Gracie are laughing about God only knows what. Pops had parked his glasses oddly on his forehead, not on top of his hair or on his nose—probably because he can't see his food with them on, but he can't see the end of the table with them off, so the forehead is a convenient place to stash them until he actually needs them.

My family is my everything, but my restaurant is my life's work.

I throw a last look back at my family, wave a quiet goodbye, and head out the front door.

I can only hope whatever's going on at the restaurant is worth leaving Sunday dinner for.

CHAPTER 8
WILLOW

THE LAST WEEK has flown by. I've been on the jobsite by sunrise nearly every day, meeting with the general contractor and supervising the last-minute decisions and approvals. I've been working out of my car, taking meetings and calls with my colleagues at Culinary Capital, and lining up final in-person talent interviews for the chefs I plan to hire for the new restaurant we're opening in Star Falls.

By the time I get back to the condo every night, unpack a few boxes, and cram some takeout into my mouth, it's a miracle I have enough energy to text my friends and brush my teeth.

Some nights, I can't even do both.

I would be lying if I said I hadn't also spent many of those precious few moments of free time regretting that I ran out on Benito. For a couple of days, I was acting like a safecracker, resting my head against the wall and listening to see if sound traveled between our units before I left my place. I've been living like a covert operative.

If I heard the faintest echo of the TV, I'd rush to the trash chute or the elevator, hoping against hope that I wouldn't run into him. When I heard the door of his unit slam in the late evenings, I knew he was home.

And I've never felt so stupid.

By Sunday, I resolve to do something about how I'm feeling.

I put on my most flattering black jeans, boots with a kitten heel, and an ultra-soft white sweater. I add delicate gold earrings, a necklace, and a casual, loose bun that I hope have me looking professional but not like I'm running into an office. I check over the notes I took from when I met Mags. She works every Sunday night. So, after a very small battle with my nerves, I check the time and call Jessa from the car.

"Still pregnant," she says, answering on the second ring. "Or did you call to talk about you?"

I chuckle. "Both."

The drive to Benito's is short, so after Jessa updates me on the adult coloring books, crying, and streaming shows she's been watching, I update her on Benito.

"I don't get it," I tell her, checking my lipstick in the mirror at a ridiculously long stoplight. "I don't get spooked by men. I don't know what the hell happened."

"That's not true," she says, and I can practically hear her shaking her head, the long, dark waves moving over her shoulders where she's propped up in bed. "You don't get serious. There's a difference. Maybe this guy hit a nerve, babe. Do you like him? Like, *like him*, like him?"

I sigh. "I don't know, Jess. We hooked up twice. I mean, I don't know enough about him to like him or not."

Jessa snorts. "I'd say any guy who can make you orgasm multiple times is more than a stranger, babe. You're starting to get to know him, at least."

I check my teeth for lipstick and then realize I'm obsessing over the stupidest little details and slam the mirror on my visor closed. "Well, I'll keep you posted. Things might get a little complicated. I think he may apply for the small business development grant Culinary Capital is sponsoring."

She sucks in a breath. "Oh, conflict can be juicy, but conflicts of interest? Never sexy."

I sigh. "Pros before bros," I chuckle. "It's kind of my thing."

"You're a pro through and through," Jessa assures me. "Maybe it's time you let one of those bros come at least as close to you as your job."

I know she means well, but I'm pulling into the restaurant parking lot. "I got to go," I tell her. "Love you. Hydrate and rest," I remind her.

"If I hydrate any more, my baby won't be the only one in diapers," she says wryly. "Love you. Call me soon. I'm almost through season three, so you know what that means…"

I shake my head and cut her off. "Jessa, you know how it ends."

"I still can't even." She blows me loud kisses over my car's speakers, and I end the call.

The parking lot of Benito's is full. I scan the lot, but I don't see Benito's SUV anywhere. Maybe he takes Sundays off? That could be why Mags works every Sunday. My shoulders sag a bit. This could be good, or this could be a sign from the universe that I should not have made this spontaneous trip on a Sunday. On the one hand, if Benny is off, I won't have to face him. But if he's not working, Mags may be too busy in the kitchen to talk to me about the grant.

Either way, I'm here. And I'm in the mood for a great meal. I gather up my purse and my courage, and I head inside.

The elderly hostess is holding court at the front of a very busy waiting area. She's sitting on a stool but hops up every few minutes to point long, painted nails or the ends of her glittery plastic glasses at someone whose table is ready.

"Darling!" she shouts over the low conversations. "Yes, I'm talking to you, Ed and Nina. Table for five is ready. Come on, now. Let's get you seated."

She motions to the people whom she obviously knows by name, jumps off her stool, and grabs an armful of menus. She notices me and nods. "Hello there, gorgeous. I'll be right back with you." But then she cocks her head at me and seems to look behind me for the rest of my party. "How many, love?" she asks. "Here for dinner?"

Nina and Ed and their kids are still gathering up toys and tying shoelaces, so I hold up one finger and nod.

"Just me," I say. "Table for one or a spot at the bar. Whatever works."

She nods and grabs another menu, motioning for me to follow. I step aside to make room for the family who I assume will sit at one of the many tables between the lobby and the bar.

As I walk through Benito's, I see table after table full. Not an empty seat in the house. This is exactly the type of crowd I would expect at a place like this on Sunday evening. Families and couples are here for Sunday dinner. Kids crying in high chairs. Teenagers slunk down in their seats, peeking at phones hidden in their laps. A table with two older women is rowdy with laughter, and the hostess points at them as we pass.

"Bev, Carol, keep it civil," she shouts, laughably louder than the women at the table. "This is a family joint."

One of the women barks a laugh and points at the hostess. "Rita, come join us when things slow down."

The hostess, whose name must be Rita, shakes her head. "No rest for us working girls, ladies." She turns to Ed and Nina before she sets the menus down on the table and gestures for them to take their seats. Then she jerks a thumb at me.

"Bar's wide open, sweetheart. Take your pick." She turns and walks back to the hostess station, so I head over to the bar and sit on the same tall stool where I was the other night.

A second later, I feel a hand at my elbow. "Excuse me." The dad from the family who was just seated hands me a menu. "I think Rita gave us one extra. This one must be yours."

"Oh wow. Thank you," I say.

He nods and heads back to his table. I'm acutely aware of the fact that I'm alone, and I'm used to it, but the sense of being out of place hits me hard. Maybe it's because everyone seems to know one another. I've worked in a few small towns before, but I've never been any place like Star Falls.

I turn back to the menu and try to focus on what I'm going to eat. I've had the dish I'm probably going to love the most, so I decide to try something new. The last thing I want to do is fall into a pattern. Some people find predictable comforting, but not me. Spinach rotolo with meatballs, it is.

The bartender I had the other night points at me and looks as if she's trying to place me. "You were here the other night?" she asks. "Restaurant lady?"

I have to laugh. After the very little small talk I'd made with the bartender, the one thing she remembered about me was that I work in restaurants. I nod. "Also known as Willow. You're Jasmine?"

She nods. "Good memory. Don't feel bad if I ask you your name the next hundred times I see you. Some days I can't keep my own kids straight."

She pours me some water, then I order an iced tea and the rotolo. "Jasmine," I add, deciding that even if now is not a good time, I should send word to Mags that I've arrived. "Could I ask you to let Mags know I'm here? I know she's probably swamped, but we met earlier this week, and I told her I'd stop back in."

"Mags?" Jasmine lifts her brows. "Yeah, sure. Happy to." But then Jasmine frowns and leans forward on the bar. "She's not looking to leave, is she? Are you here to talk to her about a job?" Jasmine looks worried and smooths down her plain black button-down shirt. "She and Benito are going through a rough patch," she says. "But he's a good man. Despite his giant you-know-what."

I almost choke on a sip of iced tea. "His giant what?" I ask.

Jasmine shakes her head. "That man's ego... He's something else." But then her eyes grow soft, and she smiles. The sounds of clinking silverware and conversation seem louder as I lean closer to hear her. "He's got an even bigger heart. I don't care what anyone says. He's a good one."

She nods at me and points to a house phone. "I'll let Mags know you're here. What's your name again?"

I remind her, giving her both my first and last name. Then I settle into my iced tea and try for the first time in a long time not to feel like such a stranger.

Mags rushes out, her hair tied back behind a bandanna and her cheeks flushed pink. She's reaching out a hand to shake mine and grinning. "Willow," she says. "I'm so glad you made it." She motions down to the empty space in front of me. "Your dinner will be right up, but I wanted to see how long you can stay. I've got—"

I hold up a hand. "It's no problem," I say. "I knew

you'd be busy. I felt like a fantastic dinner and some time with my book. I'll hang around until you have a few minutes to talk."

"Are you sure?" She looks worried. "It might be a while. Sundays can get…"

I hold up my phone. "I've got a whole library of stuff to catch up on. Take your time."

She nods and hustles back to the kitchen, and I decide to take my own advice. I flip open my e-reader and scan the dozens of titles in my library. Cookbooks and books about food science. Business books. And, of course, a couple of romance novels. I settle on a book that is high on spice and low on drama. That's what I want in my life; that's why I've got this bad boy on my bookshelf.

I sip my tea and scan the pages, growing more and more engrossed in the story of a biker who goes to prison for a stitch, but when he gets out, he meets a woman whose daughter is in distress, and I love it. Found-family vibes—my favorite kind. I'm deep into the action when a server sets a plate in front of me.

"Spinach rotolo with meatballs?" The older lady looks me over. "You need anything else, hun?"

"Sassy." The bartender waves at the woman who's brought out my dinner. "Did you meet Willow? She's a restaurant person."

My waitress, whose name I now know is Sassy, gives me a long, approving look, then grins. "You look too skinny to be a foodie." She taps a hand over her ample chest. "This is the body of a woman who knows her food."

I grin and nod at her. "I'm on the operations side," I explain. "Restaurant financing and investments. But I adore cooking and especially eating."

She nods at me. "You're in the right place. Benito's the best chef in Star Falls, but that's not saying much. Probably the best chef even in the city. You let Jasmine know if you need anything, and I'll hustle over. You want cheese?" she asks.

I nod. "Who turns down cheese?"

Sassy crows, a long, happy sound. "There's my girl. I'll be back in a second."

She rushes off, leaving a faint cloud of cigarette smoke and hair spray behind her. I haven't even looked down at my meal when I feel a light hand at my elbow.

"Willow, I'm sorry to come just as your food has arrived, but I wanted you to meet someone."

I turn at the sound of Mags's voice and crash eyes with the man I've spent all week avoiding.

Benito Bianchi.

His chocolate-brown eyes go cold, the soft stubble on his face highlighting both the dimple in his chin and his slight frown. He cocks an eyebrow at Mags.

"Mags, I don't understand…" he says, and I can tell he's struggling here.

I jump from my stool and extend a hand to him. "Mags, it turns out Benito and I have met." I hold out my hand, hoping he will shake it. "I didn't realize he was the owner when I ate here last weekend."

Benito's frown doesn't soften, but he does take my hand. He holds it carefully, like he's afraid I'm going to pull away, but it's he who pulls away first.

"I'm Willow Watkins," I say, but his touch is already gone. The heat that seared my skin leaves a chill in its path. My stomach flips, and I can feel the steady beat of my pulse hammering in my throat.

Damn. This was a bad idea. Such a bad idea.

I add a new rule to my playbook. Never sleep with a man in a too-small town. It doesn't have the same ring to it, but it's a policy I think I'm going to have to stick with. Especially if I'm going to make it through the next year.

"Nice to meet you," Benny says distractedly, but then he turns to walk away.

"Benito," Mags says pointedly, "Willow is with Culinary Capital."

He gives her a pointed glare, and I can almost see the unspoken question written all over his face. *What the fuck does that matter to me?*

Mags rushes to explain. "Willow's company is sponsoring the SBA grant. The one we're planning to apply for." She sounds so hopeful, so earnest. Like she's not only hoping that Benny remembers what she's referring to, but by putting Benny and me in the same room, we'll work some kind of finance miracle and make all the restaurant's problems go away.

I've seen it before. No matter the size of the restaurant, how well they're doing, almost every owner needs a crew that has their heart and soul in the work.

I see that in Mags. She may come off a little rough around the edges, but she cares. That's what this place needs. Whether Benito realizes it or not, Mags is an asset to his operation.

"Mags was able to attend the talk I gave at the SBA meeting earlier this week," I explain quickly. "She mentioned the restaurant's interest in applying for the grant my organization is sponsoring, and I told her I'd be happy to stop by sometime and chat a bit about writing a strong application."

"Writing a strong application," he echoes, his voice as stormy and cold as the rain that fell on us the night we met. "Let me make sure I'm following," he says, pointing to me. "Your company is in town to do what, exactly? Give away cash? What's the catch?"

Mags looks horrified and rushes in to explain. "Benito, they are opening a new restaurant in town. But they are also sponsoring a grant so the restaurants in town that will have new competition can benefit from the—"

"Whoa, whoa, whoa." Benito holds up a hand and cuts her off. "Let me get this straight. This lady here is going to open a brand-new restaurant here in town. Poach my customers, probably my staff, and who knows, maybe even my recipes." He looks down at my untouched plate of rotolo with a scowl. "But she's going to throw a little cash at my roof as a consolation prize? What is that, guilt money? So, you don't feel as bad when you put the little guys like me out of business?"

Mags's mouth has dropped open, and I'm fully standing now. "That's not exactly how we operate," I say, my voice tight.

"I know all I need to know, and I'm not interested." Benito nods at me, then he calls for Jasmine. "Jas, wrap Ms. Watkins's dinner to go. It's on the house." He turns to me and squares his shoulders. "We'd prefer if you kept your grant and your snooping as far from my restaurant as possible."

Leaving Mags, Jasmine, and me all stunned speechless, Benito turns and storms away.

CHAPTER 9
BENITO

WELL, if Mags was pissed at me before, the scales have sure as hell tilted now.

What the hell was she thinking, bringing Willow into the restaurant?

What the hell was I thinking, bringing that woman into my bed?

I've never shifted from regret to rage so fast in my life.

I pace the floors of my condo, trying to reason with myself. My mind swings from worry to worse.

Willow had said that her life was food. She actually said that she was going to try to copy my kale ravioli recipe.

My temper is about to bubble over when there is a harsh knock at my door. I can hear Willow's voice calling my name.

"Please?" She knocks again. "Benito, I just need a minute. Would you please open up?"

I ignore her. The way she's been doing to me the last

week since she ran out of here and left me with the taste of her on my lips and nothing but confusion in my chest.

Just when I think she's given up, she starts in again.

"Benito, would you please let me explain? Please. If not for my sake, for Mags's."

Hearing her say Mags's name sets my teeth on edge. I don't know what this woman's intentions are—not with me, my recipes, or my staff—but I yank open the door so I can tell her once and for all to her face to keep the hell out of my business.

When I see her standing there, she looks happy. Happy to see me. The momentary warmth on her face does a number on my anger, but only for a second.

I turn away from the soft waves falling from her bun, the light blue eyes searing into my brain.

"Come in," I tell her. "But don't get comfortable. You've got five minutes." I cross my arms over my chest, but suddenly, I can't control the rush of anxiety through my limbs.

At the sight of her, my body starts a war with my mind. I'm furious, and I should be, but the moment she closes the door, lowers her chin, and walks across the condo, it takes everything inside me to stop myself from going to her.

I've never had a hookup sink her claws into me so deep. And I've got to free myself before some real damage is done. "Five minutes," I remind her. "Then it's my turn."

She nods and looks around as if she wants to sit. I

think about being a dick and just standing there, but she looks vulnerable.

I hate it, but I motion toward my L-shaped leather sectional. "Sit," I tell her.

She nods wordlessly, then sinks down on the edge of the sofa.

I wait until she chooses a spot, then I walk to the farthest possible spot from her and sit in my recliner.

Plenty of distance between us.

No way for us to get close.

It's dark out now, and the park lights reflecting off the river cast a warm yellow glow over my place. I tap my phone and use an app to turn on a couple of lamps so we're not sitting in total darkness.

Her face is cast in shadow, the rise and fall of her breasts in the soft white sweater she's wearing seeming more and more uneven. She leans forward and wrings her hands. "I owe you an apology," she says, meeting my eyes. "I'm honestly not even sure where to start."

"Start at the beginning," I say curtly. "Or just cut to the part where you admit you're trying to steal my recipes and my business."

She shakes her head, looking confused. "What are you talking about, Benny?" She pauses after she says my name, as if it sounds as intimate to her as it does to me.

I can't make her take back the way her voice curls around every syllable.

My cock tightens behind my jeans as I remember her crying my name against my ear the first night we meet.

The way her fingers tightened in my hair as I ate her pussy.

"Just…" I stammer. "Say what you came here to say."

"Ben…Benito, I'm not what you think I am."

I can't stop baiting her. I know it's my shittiest quality. I fucking told her to talk, but I'm furious, and my body won't stop reacting to her. With every blink of her sweet blue eyes, every time she bites her lip, I want to go to her. I have to physically grab the arms of my chair to stop myself from getting up.

"So, tell me who you are, Willow. I don't know a damn thing about you. Why you're here, what you do for work. Who your family is. Are you married? What's next? You have a husband and two point three fucking kids out there someplace?"

Her expression changes then, like she's retreating inside herself. It's a look I've seen thousands of times before. On Mags's face when I push too far. On the faces of countless women I have pushed away. Something about seeing the shutters close on Willow breaks a little something inside me. I start to backtrack before I can even stop myself.

"That was out of line," I admit. "I'm sorry. I'm…" I rub my face. "I'm really fucked over here. I'm angry and a whole bunch of shit. I'm going to shut my mouth and let you speak."

She nods and then leans back a little bit into the couch. "Thank you," she says softly, her gaze never leaving mine. "I understand that you're pissed. So, thank you for letting me get a few things off my chest."

She swallows and I almost say something, but I hold the words inside and take a deep breath.

Then I wait.

"I am the chief operations officer of a restaurant investment group. About six years ago, one of our scouts ate at a restaurant in Florida. Single location, family-owned. The menu was unique, but the branding was even more unusual. We approached the family with a franchise proposal, but they didn't want to expand. Then, about two years ago, one of the grandchildren from that same family graduated from culinary school. The granddaughter wanted to open a second location, but the family didn't have the capital or the know-how. So, they came back to us."

She swallows and clears her throat, and I curse myself for not offering her water, coffee, anything. I can be furious, but I don't have to be a shit host. "You want a glass of water?" I ask.

"You said I only have five minutes," she says, a small smile on her lips.

"It doesn't take long to drink a glass of water," I say coldly, still not willing to budge.

She nods, looking a little stunned, but holds up a hand. "I'm good, thanks. I'll get this out and be on my way."

When she says that, I have to stifle the urge to tell her no, she can stay. An annoyingly persistent part of me doesn't really want her to leave.

My fucking betrayer of a body.

My brain is furious at her.

I want to know what fucking game she's playing. But

then, I don't know what I want. Her, maybe? I don't like it. I don't get it. But I get up and grab a kettle just so my hands have something to do. "You drink tea?" I ask without looking up.

"I do."

I fill the kettle to the max fill line and start the burner. Then I storm back to my chair because she's clearly going to wait until I sit down to keep talking.

"So," she says gently. "The granddaughter wanted help opening a second location. We danced around different options for ownership and viable locations to expand into." She pauses then, and I can feel her eyes on my face. I look up at her, trying to be unmoved by anything she says, anything she does. "For a lot of reasons that are proprietary, so I can't share the specifics, Star Falls was determined to be the perfect location for a second restaurant. I spent a year negotiating the deal with the family, the county, and the city. I'm here to break ground and supervise the build-out. Then when the new place is done, the granddaughter will move here to Star Falls and possess her own small part of her family's legacy."

"While Culinary Capital takes a massive cut of the profits, for what—the life of the restaurant?" I ask. I can't help myself. This doesn't sound like a good deal for anyone but Willow's business.

Willow sighs. "We signed a profit-sharing agreement that should make us whole on our investment in under thirty-six months. Our contracts have standard clauses with mutual audits and full transparency. We relinquish our investment twelve months after we're made whole. If our data and analysis are correct, the granddaughter will own the restaurant outright in as little as three years. We're not in this to screw over the little guy. My company is owned by two sisters whose father was one of the original franchisees of Papa Gino's."

She stops and meets my eyes when she shares that little fact. No wonder she ordered from them the other day and was so defensive of the mass-produced product.

She goes on. "We believe in helping communities create sustainable and profitable food industries. Sometimes that means we open franchises, and sometimes we work with people who have a gift for food but need a little support when it comes to all the other things that go into running a successful restaurant."

That fucking stings like lemon juice to the eyes. "Like me?" I demand, defensive again.

It's shockingly noble—if what she's saying is true. I've heard so many horror stories. Buddies who got taken advantage of by vendors, by real estate agents, by anyone and everyone who saw dollar signs at the first hint of their restaurants being successful. I've never heard of a finance company helping small business owners keep their businesses.

Not like this, and I don't trust it. I don't trust her.

I leap out of my chair and turn off the kettle that's just starting to steam.

Willow gets up and follows me into the kitchen. She reaches for my arm. "Benny, what I'm saying has nothing to do with you. Please, will you let me finish?"

I yank open a cabinet, pull out two mugs, and grab

the honey. "How do you take your tea?" I demand, refusing to look at her.

"Just a little honey is fine, thanks." I hear the hint of a smile in her voice, like she's laughing at what a pouty bitch I'm being. I don't give a fuck.

This woman is bad news, and I need to listen to what she's saying so I know enough to keep her the hell out of my life.

She talks while I fix our tea. "We started the SBA grant program about five years ago. It was after…" She pauses and seems to consider what she's about to say. She walks to the purse she dropped on the floor by my front door and grabs her cell phone. She swipes the touchscreen and shows me an app. "This is what we used to do."

I glare at her hand, but I finally take the teabags out of the mugs, dump them in the sink, and grab her phone. "What am I looking at?" I ask.

"In every community where we open a restaurant, we know we're going to affect the local economy. In some places, the trade-off is worth it. We create new jobs in a place that needs them. We provide opportunities for people who wouldn't have had them otherwise. For several years, when I was on the ground supervising the build of a new restaurant, I would also coordinate with the local community to give back in some very tangible way."

The social media feed she's showing me has dozens of pictures going back years. Willow is shown hugging people in community centers, test kitchens, and even in backyard fundraisers.

"We stopped the year we worked with children of incarcerated parents," she says quietly. "After that, I couldn't manage it all. The community events, the work, the people."

I see a glimmer of something real in her eyes, and it's brutal. As if, for just a second, she dropped the mask, dropped the facade, and the real Willow was laid bare. I look away from her and back at the phone. The more recent pictures show Willow at ribbon-cuttings and pig roasts.

"So, what, you give away money now? The grant is supposed to replace the community service stuff?" I ask.

She nods. "Yes. It's a newer program, but we estimate that for the additional expenditure of funds, the success of the new restaurant happens even faster. It's inevitable that some businesses will suffer and some jobs will be lost, but the goodwill and publicity the grants give us have actually helped the restaurants we open get profitable more quickly."

"Got to spend money to make money," I say acidly.

At that, Willow grabs her phone away from me, her fingers brushing mine. "You know what, Benito? I've had about enough of this pouty bullshit act. You want to know about the restaurant that you think I'm stealing recipes for? You want to know how much damage I've done to Benito's?"

She says my name a little mockingly, and for a hot second, I'm ashamed that I named my restaurant after myself. It sounds pompous as hell, especially after seeing all the good she seems to try to do. But I shove that away.

My work is my life.

I am that restaurant.

There is no me without it, and no restaurant without me. We may as well share the same name. We share the same heart, soul, and identity.

"Tell me," I say, baiting her. "Go on. You have three more minutes."

"Nice of you to keep track, but I only need one," she seethes, her anger catching up to my own. "One year from now, a Pancake Circus is going to open up. It's a family-friendly themed breakfast and brunch place. The original location in Florida is open for dinner, but our analysis led us to decide what would thrive best in Star Falls is a place that fills the need for large seasonal breakfast crowds and a consistently high-quality breakfast and brunch experience."

"Breakfast and brunch experience?" I repeat numbly. "Pancake fucking Circus?" I can't believe what I'm hearing. First of all, the place she's opening has nothing to do with Italian food, let alone dinner. So, she couldn't have been serious about stealing my recipes… could she? And second, she has a point. I've always thought Star Falls needed something better than the hole-in-the-wall strip-mall breakfast diners. I see the vision, and even worse, I don't hate it.

"It's fantastic," she says defensively. "But the good news is that in twelve months, another family will have their dreams come true, someone in Star Falls will be the recipient of a ten-thousand-dollar grant, and I will be on to the next project."

My stomach sinks.

Not just at what she's said about dreams coming true, but the grant amount. I had no idea it was that much. A chunk of cash like that would allow me to do a massive roof repair without spending a penny out of pocket. The roof could last another couple of years with a major repair job like that. The grant really could be the answer to my prayers.

But even worse, she's only here to supervise the build. She'll be gone in a year.

Two hours ago, I would have thought that was the best damn news I'd heard all week. But now, it sinks in my gut like a lead balloon.

"I'm not here to poach anything, steal anything, or cause you any grief, Benny," she says, her cheeks flushed with anger. Her blue eyes pop against the rage staining her cheeks, and I come around the counter to confront her, my anger dissipating like the steam over my mug of tea.

"So why did you run, then?" I ask, my hand on her arm. "Willow, why the fuck did you leave the other night?"

My business aside, this is what I really want to know. This is what's gutted me and eaten away at me the last week. The anger drains out of me in a rush as soon as I say the words, and I release her arm, my hands and knees feeling weak, like I've opened myself up and admitted something so big that the sheer effort has worn me down.

Willow reaches for my hand and slowly laces her fingers through mine. "I was surprised myself," she says quietly. "I think it just hit me all at once. Who you are.

That your employee had come to me for help. I felt trapped, in a way. I don't know how to be honest. I just ran. I'm sorry. I have been looking for a way to apologize all week."

I tighten my fingers around hers. "Showing up at my restaurant was probably the worst way to do it."

She nods. "I know. You've got me in knots, Benito Bianchi. I'm…" She pulls her hand away from me. "I never stay in one place for too long. I never get too attached, but I was feeling attached. You sounded attached. You said…"

I remember what I said. I have been replaying the moment in my head on a loop all week. "I know what I said," I rasp out. "I'm so glad I found you."

We're both quiet, nothing but the hushed sounds of our breaths as we consider what we've just said.

"You were just supposed to be a hookup," she says quietly. "That's all this can be."

"I don't do relationships," I tell her. "You don't have to worry about getting attached to me. It's not going to be a problem."

"What you said about finding me…"

"Forget it," I tell her. "Your pussy was in my mouth, babe. Have you tasted yourself? Of course I was fucking glad I found you."

"Are you still?" she asks, lifting her face toward mine.

"Are *you* glad?" I ask. "Do you want to be found by me?"

"For now," she says. "While I'm here in Star Falls."

"I can handle an expiration date," I tell her. "I'm actually really good with keeping things fresh."

She rolls her eyes and purses her lips. "You got any more puns I need to brace myself for?"

"Why don't you Willow Walk-er your hot ass over here?"

"No," she says, shaking her head. "Nope, nope. Never use that one again."

"All the blood's rushed to my dick," I say. "I might not be thinking straight."

I know I'm not going to regret this. My body is all in, and if there is one thing I'm great at, it's keeping my brain and my heart separate from my hookups.

I can have fun with Willow and not let it get complicated. In fact, if she's wired as much like me as I think, this may be exactly the situation I need. No strings, no long-term. Just the fun. Just the good parts.

I step forward and curl a hand around the back of her neck. "Willow," I murmur, lowering my face to her neck.

As I plant soft kisses along the column of her throat, I drink in the scent of her, the feel of her soft hair tumbling from its bun against my fingers.

"Benito," she breathes, her hands circling low to cup my ass.

I groan and press against her, my body taking over and shutting my mind down.

She may be a woman who doesn't plan to stay in Star Falls for too long, but I'll take every moment she's willing to give.

CHAPTER 10
WILLOW

THREE WEEKS LATER...

"Benito, you have to go." I wrap my legs around Benny's waist as he slides deep inside me. "Benny, fuck…"

"Shh." He leans forward and claims my lips with his. "Are you kicking me out again?"

I nibble his lower lip between my teeth and breathe him in. "Yes, again. I have a conference call in thirty minutes, and I do not need to show up looking like I just…"

A lightning bolt flashes behind my eyes as he rolls his hips, putting pressure on that sensitive spot that has me arching with need. Benny makes me greedy. He's more delicious than tiramisu, more decadent than a meal cooked by a Michelin-starred chef.

For the last few weeks, we've spent every evening together and quite a few entire nights. We fuck, we laugh, we eat, we sleep. Rinse and repeat. He's the most fun I've ever had, and yet…

A horrific series of siren sounds blare from my phone.

I flop a weak hand toward my bedside table, trying to silence my alarm.

"I have to get moving," I force out the words between his thrusts, my eyes rolling back in my head. I see darkness behind my closed lids. It's as if every inch of me is consumed by Benny. I feel him, smell him, taste him as he supports his weight on top of me and gently grinds his cock deep. My breasts are smashed under his chest, and he whispers the words against my lips between kisses.

"Come to my place after work?"

I groan, drawing in a deep breath. Even first thing in the morning, the scent of his soap, cologne, and the faintest hint of herbs from the kitchen cling to his warm skin. It's ridiculous, the effect this man has on me. I try to talk through the growing excitement that has my clit pulsing and my hips working slow circles against his. "Not tonight. I've got a video date with one of my best friends."

"After?" he asks, pulling out excruciatingly slowly and then, with a jerk of his hips, seats himself deep.

"Fuck yes, after," I pant. "After…"

I lift my hips and widen my legs, wriggling my hips and grinding up against his body until I am trembling, coming, my hands gripping his face as I kiss him.

"Fuck," I gasp into his mouth, and I feel his body tighten as my climax brings on his.

We writhe and curse, praise the heavens and moan,

until he collapses against my chest, shuddering and sweating.

Far too quickly, he covers my bare chest with kisses. "Have a great call," he says, then he starts to roll away, but I grab him and hold him tight.

"Stay a second," I tell him. I don't like shoving him off me while his heart is still thudding against mine. I stroke his hair and kiss the top of his head, thanking the gods of video conferencing that my team won't be able to smell me. A sleek bun and a black top and I can be on that call in five minutes. That leaves me five more minutes with him.

We're silent as the sweat cools between us, and Benny's limbs grow heavy on mine. "I'm stopping by my parents' today," he says. "And Mags is closing the kitchen, so I'll probably be home by eight. You want to eat together after your call, or will that be too late?"

"Depends," I murmur into the thick waves of his hair. "Who's cooking?"

He chuckles. "Your choice. I've been working on a new recipe, and I'd love a guinea pig."

"Deal," I say. "Your place, my palate."

"Your mouth," he growls, kissing me again. Then he rolls off the bed, slides the condom off, and wanders into my bathroom to toss it out. I watch his bare ass as he goes, his cock still hard. His thighs are thick and hairy, and I feel a grin cross my face as I watch him. He dresses in a miraculously short amount of time and then holds out his hand to me. "Come on, gorgeous. Unless you're planning on takin' that call from bed?"

I grab his hand, and he kisses the tip of my nose after I climb out of bed.

"Lock the door behind me," he calls out, releasing me and heading for the front door.

I grab the sheet, which is halfway on the floor anyway, wrap it around myself, then stand behind the door while Benny lets himself out and walks to his condo next door. He looks back at me, gives me a feral grin, and then goes inside his place.

As soon as he shuts his door, I lock mine, drop the sheet, and run for the bathroom. I check the time. I have like five minutes to make myself look like I didn't just have two orgasms. Easy peasy.

I throw on a work top and fix my hair, then while I brush my teeth, I pull up the agenda for the call. Odd, but there is no agenda. Just a "status chat" with the strategic team back in Chicago. I shrug. I can provide status reports without any prep, so I hope this is a short but sweet call.

I'd really like to shower sooner rather than later. Not that I'm anxious to get the scent of Benny's sweat off my skin, but if tonight goes like the last few nights have, I won't have to wait long to taste and smell him again.

I grab my laptop and set up at the kitchen counter with the morning light over the river illuminating my face. I look happy. And I'm sure it's more than just the orgasms from Benny. Everything in my life right now is going perfectly. I have a man in my bed who gets me, people in my life who love me, and work that thrills me.

Things are perfect.

I fire up the laptop with a grin on my face, but it dies as soon as I see Alexandra's face.

"What's going on?" I ask, without even saying good morning. "You all look like someone shit in your coffee. What's happened?"

"How are things in Star Falls, Willow?" Alexandra, my administrative assistant, is the only one who isn't muted. "I'm giving everyone a moment to get oriented before I open the meeting to Theresa."

"Theresa?" I ask.

Theresa Ginetti and her sister Rosemarie are the founders of Culinary Capital, the daughters of the Papa Gino's pizza franchise. They are hands-on owners, but having one of them attend a routine status call is *not* normal.

Something is going on.

Something big.

"Yes. Theresa," Alexandra says softly. "She'll be joining us today."

Before I ping Alex with a private chat message and ask her what the hell is up, the Zoom room comes into view as all the attendees are let in. In total, there are seven people on camera, including me.

"Good morning, Willow." Theresa addresses me by name first, then checks in with each of the staff members on the call.

It takes a moment or two for her to greet each of us, but it's a habit she's gotten into, and it's one I appreciate. We're a small company in terms of staff, and having the founders know each of us by name, know exactly what we're doing, is the kind of business that sets us apart from our competitors. Even though I'm itching to know why we're all here—an all-hands meeting with no agenda, by the looks of it—I'm not sensing any bad-bad vibes.

I think about texting Alex, but her eyes look glued to the camera, like she has no idea what's up either. She looks even more scared than I feel.

Theresa quickly puts the questions in the air to rest. "So," she says, her face strained by a tense smile. "I have some news that I wanted to deliver myself."

My stomach sinks.

I don't know what kind of not-good news Theresa would deliver herself, but I rest my hands on the cool marble counter and brace myself.

An image of Benny flashes in my mind. I wonder if he'll be free after this call. I'm going to want to talk to someone, work through whatever this is, and even though this thing between us is new and has an expiration date, I already feel like he's someone I can talk to.

But thoughts of Benny fade away the moment I hear Theresa's announcement. "The Pancake Circus franchise deal has hit a wrinkle. More than a wrinkle. A wall."

Theresa's eyes seem to be looking right into the camera. I feel like she's staring directly at me. She shakes her head. "It's not the first time this has happened with a deal, but it is the first time this has come up on one of your deals, Willow."

My stomach sinks even lower, like a stale biscuit dropping to the bottom of an empty trash bin. I swallow against the sour taste in my mouth and nod. "Okay," I say. "What happened? What can I do?"

Theresa explains that the granddaughter who'd wanted to open the Ohio location wants out.

"Out?" I shake my head. "The deal has been signed. We've broken ground on the renovation. We're three weeks into the build-out. There's no getting out of this deal."

Theresa sighs. "I know. Our lawyers are swapping letters, so for now, no changes. Business as usual. But I wanted you to have a heads-up." She runs a hand down her cheek, her expression a little sad. "I'm trying to get to the bottom of this amicably, but their lawyers have told me that whatever is going on in Florida is serious enough that the family is considering filing suit."

"A lawsuit? Against us?" I shake my head. "They can't do that. On what basis? What about the mediation provision?"

Our contracts take years to conclude, and every single one includes a long dispute resolution provision. Before anyone can sue anyone, everyone who is party to the agreement is bound to first try mediating the issues, which is basically a much less expensive process that would avoid the hundreds of thousands in legal fees and years of delays that a lawsuit would involve.

"I know that, Willow." Theresa sounds tired. "They must be incredibly upset to already be talking litigation."

"I can't believe this," I say, the reality of the situation sinking in. "I was involved in every phone call, every Zoom meeting, every on-site visit with the family. They wanted this second location. We didn't put pressure on them. For God's sake, they came to us."

"Willow." Theresa shakes her head and rubs a weary hand across her brow. "I know that. You didn't do anything wrong. Something has happened, and…" She sighs. "Rather than calling us, they ran to their lawyers."

"Have you called them?" I ask. "Voice to voice, to ask what's going on?" I already know the answer to this question, but I want to know if Theresa even tried.

"I can't call them now. You know that I can't." Theresa again shakes her head.

If the family has already retained a lawyer, it would be unethical for someone from Culinary Capital to speak to them directly.

If Theresa wants to contact them, the only thing she can do now is go through their attorneys.

"And we have no idea what changed? Why, all of a sudden, they just want out?" Acid is burning in my stomach, and I am half tempted to take myself off camera and go find some antacids.

If a lawsuit is filed, the first thing that will happen is the Pancake Circus family, the Kincades, will file an emergency injunction. That will stop us from building or spending any money or moving forward in any way on the second location. I know that because it's happened to Culinary Creations exactly two times in the years I've worked here. Just never on a project that I was responsible for.

"I'll share more when I know more," she says, nodding. "I'm going to excuse myself for my next meeting, but Willow, I've asked their attorney to provide a formal demand letter explaining exactly what they want within two weeks. I'll keep you posted."

"And what should I do in the meantime?" I ask. "Business as usual?"

Theresa sighs, and she sounds as frustrated as I feel. "I wish I could say yes, but until we know what the problem is, I'd like you to slow down what you can. If they haven't provided a written demand in two weeks, we'll regroup and I'll loop in counsel so we know we're doing what we can to protect ourselves. Thanks, everyone."

Theresa disappears from the call, leaving the six of us staff members quiet and looking lost. My assistant, Alex, immediately asks, "What can I do, Willow? Should I contact some of the contractors?"

"I'll do it," I tell her. I'm tremendously grateful for her, and the offer is so sweet, so generous. But this is something I have to handle personally. "It's better that it come from me."

Suddenly, something else hits me. "Alex," I say, "I just thought of something I should have asked Theresa. I've already announced through the local SBA that the community development grant is open for applications. Should I shut that down? I need to know if she's going to honor the grant if we pull out of Star Falls."

Alex nods. "On it," she says.

The rest of the team gives their condolences to me, letting me know they feel terrible and they're happy to help with anything they can do. I love my team. We're like family in so many ways. But there is nothing they can do. This is something I have to face myself.

After the Zoom is over, I chomp down three antacids and make some tea, then take the world's hottest shower while I try not to panic.

This is just business.

I angle the rainfall showerhead so it envelops my face and hair with hot water. I hold my breath, then let it out slowly, letting the delicious steam soften the tightness in my shoulders. I lather my hair, trying to work out what could have happened.

I can't understand what went wrong. I truly can't believe this deal might end. A lawsuit could tie up the company for years in expensive litigation. All that time wasted. Money wasted.

By the time I've shaved my legs and rinsed my hair, I'm fuming mad.

I know business is business, but I've never had a deal go south. And I'm not going to stand by and let this one fizzle away, costing my company hundreds of thousands of dollars in lost profits and legal expenses. All the contracts we've signed. But this deal falling apart won't just cost hundreds of thousands. At the end of the day, this could be a seven-figure catastrophe for my company —with my name all over it.

I wrap myself in a towel and rage-dry my hair. As I'm brushing my teeth, I grab my phone and think about texting Benny. My gut wants to vent to him. Tell him what's going on. But if this deal falls apart, I'll be leaving Star Falls.

The longer I think about it, the more enraged I am. I have to stop myself from stomping all over the condo because I might have downstairs neighbors still at home.

I'm dressed in jeans and eating some yogurt in front of my laptop when I get an instant message on our corporate messaging system from Alex.

Alex: Theresa says yes, keep the grant open. If we go to litigation, we'll include the grant as damages.

Damages.

Fuck.

I message her back, but my heart's not feeling very thankful.

Me: Thanks so much, A.

Enraged, I sort through my emails for the contact number I have for the granddaughter of the founder of Pancake Circus. The woman who wanted this deal to go through and who now wants out.

I find not only her email but her personal cell phone. I grab my phone, punch in the number, and without hesitating, hit call.

Theresa may not be able to call her as long as she has an attorney, but I'm the one who met with this woman countless times. I'm the one who listened to her —in our offices back in Chicago—when she changed her mind and decided she wanted to pursue her dreams of owning her own place. I'm the one who championed this deal with Culinary Capital. If she wants out, I'm the one she should be explaining herself to.

It rings once, twice, and then a third time.

"Hello?" A hurried-sounding voice that most definitely does not belong to Audrina Kincade answers.

"Hello, may I speak with Audrina, please?" I try not to sound pissed. I try to sound professional. Pleasant, even.

"She can't come to the phone right now," the voice on the other end says. "Can I tell her who's calling?"

I hesitate, but instead of saying the company, I just give her my name. "This is Willow Watkins."

"Just a moment, please." The woman must not even set the phone down because I hear a muffled sound, and then she calls to Audrina.

I can hear the conversation almost as clearly as if I'm on speaker.

"It's who?"

That's Audrina. I recognize her voice.

"Willow? Do you have a friend Willow, honey? I don't know who that is…"

Whoever answered Audrina's phone is not her mother, and she doesn't sound old enough to be her grandmother. Where the hell is she, and who is answering her phone?

"Come on," I beg, whispering my prayer to the heavens. "Just talk to me, Audrina. Just come to the phone."

But then I hear Audrina's voice as if she's right there in the same room with me.

"Willow is the restaurant woman," she hisses. "From Culinary Capital. Hang up. Just hang up on her."

And the next thing I know, after a flurry of sounds, the call goes silent.

So much for talking to Audrina.

Just as I'm about to accept defeat, I see an email pop up from Theresa marked confidential and proprietary. I open it immediately and read it out loud.

Kincade family attorney has agreed to give me a demand letter within two weeks. Stand down until then. Slow as much work as you can without alarming the contractors. If we can resolve this, I don't want to fall too far behind. Stall the grant, but we'll honor it. Just sit tight. We'll know more in two weeks.

Thank you, team.

Theresa

I drop my head into my hands. Two weeks. We'll know more in two weeks. Which probably means Audrina will tell her attorney that I tried calling her, and that, no doubt, will get back to Theresa. But I don't care. This is all I've worked for over the last two years. There is no reason for this deal to fall apart.

I may be stalled, but I'm damn well not going on vacation. I'm going to do everything in my power to make Pancake Circus happen.

CHAPTER 11
BENITO

I'M PARKING on the street in front of my parents' house when my pops comes out the front door. He's carrying Grace's son in his arms and manages to juggle the toddler in one hand so he can wave.

I climb out of the SUV and point at little Ethan. "Little man. Got a hug for your favorite uncle?"

My dad blows air through his lips, laughing at my boast. "Don't tell Vito and Franco that this one's your favorite." He sets Ethan down on the driveway, and the little guy toddles up to me so fast, he stumbles over a pair of ridiculously cute shoes. I swoop in fast and scoop him up before his knees hit the ground.

"Whoa. Look at those reflexes, huh? Uncle Franco is too old for that kind of action, and Vito..." I shake my head and then tap the end of Ethan's nose. "Vito's just not that sharp." I point to myself. "Say it with me—Benny is the best."

My pops shakes his head while I blow raspberries into the little guy's neck. Ethan screams with laughter and kicks his little feet, then wriggles out of my arms and army-crawls up the driveway toward his grandpop.

"Where's Ma?" I ask, leaning over to kiss my dad's cheek.

"Inside," he says. "She's sewing something for Eden and Juniper."

"They're here too?" I ask, a little irritated.

My parents' place is like an open house almost every day of the week, but sometimes I wish I could have a few minutes alone with them. There's never enough of Mario and Lucia to go around, and I'd really like to have some time to talk to my ma alone. Maybe even both of them.

Pops nods. "Everybody's in V's room."

Vito moved out of my parents' house and into a house he shares with Eden almost a year ago, but my parents still call his bedroom Vito's room. Even though it's now a dedicated craft room for my mom. Hell, my parents have converted every one of our bedrooms to serve some new purpose, and yet they still refer to them as our rooms. It's just one of the ways they let us know that we still have a place under their roof. It's about more than being family. It's about always knowing we can go home. I pray I never need to, but there's something really comforting about knowing I have a place to land no matter how life pulls the rug out from under me.

While Pops and Ethan head to the backyard to play catch, I kick off my shoes and head to see Ma. As I walk into the house, I smell something delicious and unusually sweet. I make a stop in the kitchen and see a cooling rack covered in un-iced cinnamon rolls on the counter.

I give them an appreciative sniff, pour myself a cup of coffee, and take a few sips before heading upstairs.

No matter how long it's been since I lived here, I respect the house rules. Shoes off. No cursing—which none of us can manage to do, no matter how old we get, but we try—and no food or drinks in the bedrooms.

I set my coffee cup on the counter and am about to head up the stairs when I get a text.

Mags: Did you sign off on the application?

No greeting, no good morning, just a question. I sigh and tap out a quick reply.

Me: It's on my list for this week. Will get to it.

The truth is, the application for the Culinary Capital community development grant has been done for two weeks. Mags met with Willow at some point—I don't know when and, to be honest, didn't want to know—and filled out all the paperwork for me. All I have to do is complete the financials, because I don't give anyone access to my books but me, and sign.

But I've been dragging my feet. Willow has assured me that she has nothing to do with making the final decision about the grant. She has never been anything other than a goodwill ambassador, basically talking up the grant and spreading the word, trying to soften the blow to the community when a new restaurant opens up and creates competition for the rest of the businesses out there.

But something inside me feels weird about asking for charity. Especially from someone I'm sleeping with.

Yeah, we could use the cash and I definitely need the new roof, but the grant application isn't due for another week. I don't know why getting it in early means so much to Mags, but she's been riding me like she's personally expecting to get the cash if we're awarded the grant.

I check my phone. There's no response to my text, although I see the little text bubble like she's about to send me back a message, but nothing comes. Mags is either pissed or has accepted my answer.

I head up the stairs and hear Ma baby-talking to Junie.

"Who looks like a little princess?" she asks. "Look at you. You're such a big girl."

I peek my head in the door of Vito's old room. Eden is sitting on his bed, and Ma is sitting at her sewing machine. Juniper, who is about the same age as Ethan, is twirling in a very brightly colored mini-cheerleader costume.

"Yo, yo," I say, winking at Eden.

"Hey, Benny," she says, smiling. She gets up from the bed and clasps me in a quick hug.

I bend down to kiss my ma's head and then kneel down to meet Junie at eye level. "What's this?" I ask. "Halloween costume?"

Eden laughs. "Worse. Junie is obsessed with the cheerleaders at my work. Your mom decided she needed her own cheerleading uniform."

My sister Grace's husband runs a kids' athletic facility, but I had no idea they had cheerleaders. "We talking kiddie cheerleaders or grown-ups?"

"Benny." My mother smacks my arm and pushes sparkly red reading glasses up off her nose. "The *kids* are the cheerleaders."

Eden snorts. "Running out of prospects?"

I almost curse, but then look from my mom to June and say, "No, and I'm not looking either."

Eden lifts her brows, and even my ma looks intrigued.

"Son, you have someone special?" Ma jumps out of her chair just as Juniper tries to do a handstand on the floor by herself. "Whoa, whoa, sweetheart. Wait for Nonna."

Ma kneels down on the floor by Junie while I wave a hand. "It's casual," I say, searching for the right words.

I don't have to explain because Eden answers for me. "You only do casual, right?" There's no judgment in Eden's question, and unlike my siblings, she isn't teasing me. She sounds genuinely interested.

"Ah." I wave a hand, brushing the question away. No point in analyzing my love life with my brother's girlfriend. Or anyone, for that matter. I know I'm the last in the family to settle down, and what's the rush? "I'm married to a sexy beast of a restaurant. That's more than enough commitment in my life."

"If there is someone," my ma says gently, "even if it is casual, you know you can always bring her to Sunday dinner. We'd love to be more involved in that part of your life. You need someone to care for you. To be there for you, Benny. You work so much, and…"

I look my ma over. She looks concerned, like maybe

she's overstepping by asking about that part of my life. I love her for it.

There's never been a girl I've brought home—not since high school, and that doesn't exactly count.

I know I have a reputation in my family for fucking anything that moves and never staying with one woman for too long. And I know my parents worry. I certainly don't want them worrying about or even thinking about my love life.

"Ma, don't worry, okay? I'm fine. I've got plenty of people to care about me. And I'm in no rush for one of these of my own," I say, holding out my arms to Junie. She lifts her arms and demands that I pick her up, so I do then spin around with her in my arms, making the pleats of her tiny cheerleader skirt whirl. She cackles and drools on my arm, and then I catch a whiff of what's happening in her diaper, which is my cue to hand her to her mom.

"When do they learn to use the bathroom?" I ask, wrinkling my nose.

"Not soon enough." Eden grabs her backpack and heads toward the bathroom with Junie while I chuckle.

I'm still waving a hand in front of my assaulted nose when Ma sits back down at the sewing machine.

Since it looks like we have a minute alone, I lower my voice. "So, Ma, what's the latest with the old man?" I ask.

She blinks her deep brown eyes, loaded with sparkly silver eyeshadow, at me and shakes her head. "He hasn't said anything. Maybe I should stop worrying, I don't…"

Just then, we hear Pops on the stairs. "Lucia!" he

yells. "I've got a grandson who is dying for one of these cinnamon rolls. We got plans to frost these any time soon?"

I extend a hand to my mother and help her up. She gives me a hug and murmurs, "My boy. My heart." Then she looks up at me, her lashes blinking fast. "Maybe no news is good news. Let's go eat."

I hear Eden running water in the bathroom, so it's time to put this conversation on pause anyway. I'm about to follow my ma down the stairs when my phone rings. The caller ID reads *Benito's*.

"This is Benny," I say, not sure who from the restaurant would be calling, but I check the time on my watch.

"Benny, it's Jasmine."

"Hey, Jas. Everything all right?" I stomp downstairs, hoping Ma's whipping up some cream cheese frosting for those rolls. If not, I may have to do that myself.

The entire family gathers in the kitchen, and I'm trying to hear what Jasmine's saying.

"Mags…" I barely make out over the chatter of my parents and the babbling of the kids. "So, what do you want me to do?"

"Hold up, Jas. I can't hear you." I give up on trying to take this call with my family around, so I head to the living room and drop down on a couch. "Sorry. I'm at my folks'. Hit me with that again?"

Jas huffs a sigh. "I know you're supposed to be off today, but Mags called out. What do you want to do?"

"Wait, wait." The blood starts to boil in my veins. Mags *just* texted me, and now she's calling out on the night she's supposed to close? "Did you talk to Mags? What do you mean, she called out?"

Jas hesitates a minute. "I don't know, Benny. I don't want to get in the middle of anything. She just called and said she couldn't come in tonight and she'd work it out with you later."

"Why the fuck didn't she just call me?" I ask, my voice rising along with my temperature. Thankfully, Ma didn't hear the f-bomb I just dropped or the one I was about to.

"Who's covering lunch?" I ask. "Who's there right now?"

I check the time on my phone. It's only eleven, so we're about to hit the lunch rush. Mags was scheduled to work from noon to nine today.

"Carla and Duncan are covering lunch. Mags just called me about ten minutes ago."

"She called you?" I'm barely able to control my temper.

"Well, the restaurant, Benny. The kitchen's swamped, so I answered the call."

I tighten my grip on my phone. There's only one conclusion I can jump to, and I know it's a dangerous one. Did Mags text me before the start of her shift to see if I'd signed that application? Did she intentionally call out to punish me for not doing it? And to not call me like a chickenshit, when she knows the kitchen can't run through both a lunch service and a dinner with the same crew? I'd be stuck paying overtime for one, and that's assuming Carla and Duncan would be willing to work through close.

This means Mags knew today was my day off, and she decided not to let me know I'd need to come in. She's fucking with me. That's the only explanation.

What doesn't make sense is why. Benito's is my fucking restaurant. If she needs reminding, I'll march her right out front to the parking lot and show her exactly whose name is on the fucking sign.

"I'm on my way," I tell her. "If you hear back from Mags, you tell her to call me. No. Forget that, Jasmine. I'll tell her my fucking self."

Thank God I showered after the fuckfest I had with Willow this morning. I have more clothes in my office, so there's nothing stopping me from heading right into work. I open up my contacts and pull up my last text to Willow.

Me: Day went to shit, babe. I've got to close the kitchen tonight. Late late dinner or rain check?

I have a reply back in seconds.

Willow: Day went to shit here today too. I'll cook for you tonight. My place? As soon as you can?

I send her back a thumbs-up emoji, then head into the kitchen. I reach past Pops and pull the only frosted cinnamon roll off the display plate. "Can I grab and go? I'm sorry, but Mags called out. I got to go in."

My pops waves at me to eat, while Ma starts scurrying, trying to make me a plate of the food she's cooked Eden and the kids for lunch.

"Ma, I'm a chef. I'm going to the restaurant. I'll eat, I promise." I jam a bite of the treat into my mouth and talk around a mouthful of food, mostly because I know it'll rile my mother up. "Duhlishush, Ma."

"Oh, get out of here," she says, smirking and waving me off.

Pops walks me to the door and rests a hand on my shoulder. "I'm so proud of you, Benny," he says.

There's something quiet in his voice, and I'm again hit with the realization that I don't really know what's going on with my parents. Just because Pops hasn't been back to the doctor, or at least he hasn't brought it up, doesn't mean that he's okay. That there isn't something simmering that could make the precious little time we have together even more precious.

I can't think that way. Not now.

I nod and swallow a wave of tough emotions. "Later, Pops," I say, wishing I could say more, but not knowing what or even how to say it.

I climb behind the wheel of my SUV. When Pops goes back inside, I dial Mags's number.

Ring.

Ring.

No answer.

The voice mail picks up, and I hang up before I can start cussing into the phone. I don't need to have that kind of unprofessional evidence out there. I take a few deep breaths and start up the truck. What should I do? Call? Text?

My head is starting to throb. This is the kind of shit Mags normally helps me with. When we have asshole college kids who blow off work, or when a new line chef decides to get a little sloppy with the time clock, Mags intervenes, playing good cop so I can play bad. I hardly ever have to deal with the messy personal shit because

Mags is so good at it. I squint my eyes closed and curse the fact that I've relied on someone else for so much.

What would Mags do? Would she call and leave a scathing message, swearing and blowing off steam?

No. She'd pick up the phone and leave a professional and clear message.

So, I dial her number again. This time, it goes straight to voice mail.

She's probably screening my call, but I'm going to handle this like the owner of a business. Like a man who can handle shit and get it done right.

I think about what I know Mags would say and then what I want to say. So what comes out of my mouth when the voice mail invites me to leave a message is somewhere in the middle.

"Mags, it's Benito. Jas just told me you called out. You texted me this morning, so I had no reason to think my day off would get fucked up, but now I'm going in to cover for you. I'm not going to lie. I'm pissed. Whatever's going on, not calling me is just plain shitty. You know it and I know it. But I'll get over it. What I really want to tell you is that I need to know what's really going on. If you're mad at me or trying to punish me for something, let's get it out in the open. I'm your boss and your backup, and I deserved better. But I'm going to handle it. I'd just like to know if this is the new normal I should expect, or if there's some other conversation we need to have."

Before I hang up, I see the curtains part. Ma is looking at me, and even at this distance, I can see the concern on her face. It occurs to me that maybe something is going on with Mags that I don't know about. That she's not ready to talk about, even to me.

"And shit, Mags," I say, softening my tone. "We've worked together a long time. I'm pissed, but I'm also worried. We're friends, right? So, whatever is going on, call me direct. Let's sort it out."

I hesitate, and before the silence of the dead air on the voice mail system cuts me off, I end the call.

It wasn't pretty, but it was honest. And that's the best I can offer. I guess I'll see if it's good enough.

CHAPTER 12
WILLOW

I AM TUCKED between Benny's legs, leaning my bare back against his naked chest. He's got his arms around me, my breasts cupped in his hands. As we talk, he lazily squeezes and strokes my boobs.

I can feel his hard cock behind me, but I'm trying to focus on what he's saying and not on what our bodies have spent the last few hours doing and should already be tired of but are not.

"This whole Mags thing," he mutters. "I don't get it. She's always been my right hand. I don't understand why she's pissed all the time." He's quiet for a moment, and I try to focus on his words and not the heat of his palms on my sensitive flesh. "I hate this feeling," he rumbles. I can feel the truth of his words, the vulnerability he's exposing radiating from his chest.

Something about not looking me in the face, but talking to the top of my head, has Benny opening up. As much as my body is in delicious agony, I can't turn off my brain. Not when he's talking about real stuff like this.

"What feeling?" I press. "What do you hate?"

He's quiet, and his hold on my breasts tightens. "I feel like nothing I do is good enough."

He falls silent, and I follow his lead. I want to ask more, want him to say more, but I feel his dick soften behind me, so I know he's lost in thought.

"I am not the easiest person to work with," he admits. "And I haven't always made the best decisions for the business. But I'm always straight with my people. I tell it like it is. No means no, yes means yes. I don't play games. At least, I don't think I do."

He's quiet, and I lace my hands through his so I can touch him. His arms are heavy and warm around me, and I lean my head back against his chest. We sit there quietly, our clasped hands resting together on my belly.

"What do you think Mags needs?" I ask. "Most of the time when people are angry at work, there's a really simple explanation. They want more money, more respect. Do you think she's feeling unappreciated?"

Benny sighs, and the soft heat of his breath ruffles my hair. "Maybe. Probably. I don't know."

I nod and give what I know of the situation some thought. "Have you asked her? I know you need to address the fact that she called out tonight without even contacting you, but what if you set that aside for a minute. Just ask her what she needs from you as a boss. As a leader in the place where she spends a lot of time and gives a ton of her energy. Have you ever done that?"

Benny is quiet, and I pull one of my hands away so I can stroke the long, tight muscles of his thigh. Beside mine, his body looks so hairy and thick. Strong where I'm slight. We look beautiful together, and it's hard to sit here and see the lines of his perfect body without touching it.

He gives a slight groan, but I'm not sure if it's because of my massage or my question. "I do annual evaluations and shit, if that's what you mean. I don't have an HR department or anything, but I give raises and reviews. Mags has to know how much she means to me."

"Maybe it's more than that." My mind drifts to the Pancake Circus family. I've been giving the whole situation a ton of thought. I should say I've been spiraling about this all damn day.

I just cannot imagine why they would back out, but the longer I think about it, the more I realize there are things that I need to know, need to do. I cannot let this go into litigation. There has to be a way to work out whatever it is that's happening. I wish, more than anything, that Audrina would have picked up the phone, and taken my call. I tried to do exactly what I'm telling Benny to do. I'm sure it'll work since it's not like Mags won't speak to him. She just didn't answer his call today.

"You never really know what's going on with someone," I remind him. "Sometimes you have to ask. But if you do ask, you have to be ready to deal with whatever the answer is."

He kisses the top of my head and doesn't say anything.

I shift slightly so I can meet his eyes. "Is it money?" I ask. "Do you think this has anything to do with the grant?" I feel a little sick at the question.

I believe the grant is important to Mags. Important enough that she came to the SBA meeting. She met with me separately at the restaurant to talk about it. I haven't done a lot of talking with Benny, despite all the fucking we've done, but I don't get the sense he's even half as interested in the grant as Mags seems to be.

Benny shrugs. "I wish I knew what she wants. I don't have a fucking clue." His handsome face grows dark, and he nods at me. "What about you? How's Pancake Circus treating you?"

Now, it's my turn to sigh. "Not a whole lot better than you're doing."

Benny wraps his arms around me and holds me tight against his chest. "Want to talk about it?"

His voice purrs against my ear, and I think about it. I really do. But if I tell him there's a chance this deal won't go through, that I'll get pulled out of Star Falls... I know this is a no-strings situation. I know we've only been hooking up for three weeks. I know all of that. But that doesn't mean I'm willing to give him up. I want him for as long as I can have this. And when I can't, well, then it will be time to deal with goodbyes. But nothing puts a damper on short-term fun like long-term realities.

"You know what I'd like more?" I ask, turning around and kneeling between his legs. "I'd like you to fuck me until I forget I even have a job."

His brown eyes sparkle, and the corner of his mouth

curls up in a seductive grin. "I never knew that was an option. New achievement unlocked."

"It's not an achievement until you do it," I remind him.

He puts his hands on either side of my face and leans forward. When his lips touch mine, I let myself go, lose myself in the heat and delicious sweetness of his full lips, the scrape of the stubble on his chin against mine. I open my mouth to kiss him, and his tongue sweeps against mine.

"Willow," he groans against my mouth. "I want to fuck you so many ways I can't decide where to start."

I pull back from the kiss and settle on my belly between his legs. "Think about it," I tease, pressing my lips to the head of his cock. "I'll keep myself busy until you decide."

I grip the base of his cock in one hand and suck his head into my mouth. I swirl my tongue around every tender inch of skin, paying special attention to the underside of his shaft. I suck him in deeper, licking and sucking, my hand sliding up and down his shaft. I pull my mouth back to take a deep breath of air and lick my palm so it slides against his erection without any friction. He gasps, his hips bucking, and I take him deep into my mouth again until he laces his hands through my hair and gently tugs.

"Up here," he demands. "I want you to fuck me."

He rests his head back against my headboard, and I straddle his hips. Bracing my hands on his shoulders, I don't slide onto him, but sit on his thighs. I reach for the bedside table and open a drawer, only to come up with a completely empty box of condoms.

"Uh-oh," I say, shaking the empty box. "Small problem."

Benny groans. "I have some at my place…"

I think for a moment. This is the worst possible time to have this conversation, or maybe it's the best?

"Should we talk about going without?" I ask him. "I have been on the birth control pill for two years to help with my fluctuating hormones. Aging is a bitch. I get tested every year when I have my annual physical, and I haven't gone without a condom in a long-ass time. Is it something we should consider?"

"I'm good with the birth control pills, but babe, why are you testing your hormones?"

I shake my head. "Benny, I'm forty-two. Will be forty-three this summer and it's not uncommon to start menopause at my age."

His eyes widen, and then a slow grin covers his face. "You're forty-two?" he asks, sounding incredulous. "Forty-two? As in forty-two whole-ass years old?"

I climb off his lap and give him a look. "Why? Does it matter? How old did you think I was?"

He reaches for me and pulls me closer. "Willow, you look…I don't know, mid-thirties."

"Forty-two isn't young, but it isn't old," I insist.

He holds up his hands. "It isn't. I get it, but you're older than me by a lot."

My stomach sinks. I honestly never thought about whether Benny would care how old I am. What does an age difference matter if this is just a casual fling? But then I start to panic. How young is he?

"What's a lot?" I ask. "Are you over forty?"

He shakes his head. "Thirty-one, sweetheart."

My shoulders sag. "You're a baby." What I mean, though, is he's young enough to have never been married. To never have had kids. Most of my friends are through their first marriages. Some are on their second divorces. A couple have young kids, but a lot more have kids who are already in middle school. All of that is ahead for Benny. There's no reason why he should spend the next however much time with someone he could definitely not have any of those things with.

"I'm hardly a baby," Benny says. "But you're probably not going to have kids, then?"

A cold chill creeps up the back of my neck. This is why I keep things casual. This is why I don't stay with one guy or in one place for too long.

"I don't want children," I tell him, unable to keep the edge from my voice. "I never have. My age has nothing to do with that."

He's quiet, studying my face in a way that makes me feel exposed. I reach for the sheets and wrap myself up. He doesn't say anything, just waiting, I guess, for me to explain myself. I shouldn't have to explain myself. Not having kids, not wanting to be a mother, shouldn't be something I have to defend. Not to anyone. And yet, it feels like I owe this to him. I hate that feeling.

Benny must read the look on my face, or maybe it's the way I've pulled back and wrapped myself up.

Because the next thing I know, he's kneeling on the bed and taking me in his arms.

"Hey," he says. "Come here."

He sits back against the headboard and holds me, still wrapped in the sheet, in his arms.

"I had an amazing childhood," he offers. "Two amazing parents. Three older siblings who adore the shit out of me. They can be assholes, but they're my assholes." He chuckles. "Truth be told, there's so much chaos in my life with my business, I don't know if I have enough energy for a relationship, let alone parenthood."

I listen, not sure what he's getting at.

"I don't know if I ever want kids," he says. "I love my family and they mean everything to me, but…" He shrugs. "Willow, I don't care how old you are. I don't care if you're past your childbearing years." He releases me only to make air quotes around childbearing. Then he wraps me up in his heat again. "I fucking love whatever this is we're doing. And I'm okay to keep doing it, without condoms, as long as you feel safe to."

I turn to look at him, his seductive grin turning my insides to hot jelly.

"Is it weird that I kind of love the fact that I'm banging a cougar?"

"How about we not call it anything?" I ask, my shoulders softening. "We're two grown adults, two consenting adults, and…"

I stop when he takes my face in his hands. "Yes, we are. Enough about the age gap, the kids shit… Now, can we get back to doing what we do best? Just being us?"

"Just being us," I echo. That is what I want. Easy. Fun. Light. "I think I can do that."

"So, are we being us with condoms or without?" he asks. "Because I'll walk down the hall naked and grab some from my place if that's what it takes."

I stifle a laugh. "I'm not about to let any of the other women in this building see what they're missing out on. All of this is mine for now."

For now.

The words rise between us like a wall, but Benny doesn't seem to notice or care.

"I'm all yours, babe," he agrees, then grabs my face and pulls me close.

Now our kisses are frenzied, his tongue hot and searching. The sheet falls away from my shoulders, and I don't know if he's yanked it away or if I've shrugged it off, and I don't care. I'm so hot for Benny. Hot for younger-than-me, impulsive, hothead Benny. This is all mine, and even if *for now* means weeks and not the months to one year that I'd planned, I'd rather have what I can get of him than let any of this go.

We kiss, kneeling on the bed until we collapse, Benny lying on his back and me straddling him. But he seems to have other ideas.

"Lie back," he says. "I want a taste."

I close my eyes and lose myself in the gentle kisses, until I feel his palms open my thighs wider.

I arch my hips, aching to feel any part of him inside me. He kisses my pussy, licking and stroking my clit, bringing me agonizing, beautiful pleasure but never entering me.

I roll my hips, I tear my fingers through his thick hair, but he never moves his mouth from my pussy. I'm ready to explode when I feel a rush of cold air as he moves away.

"No," I grunt, not wanting him to stop, but praying that he's moving because he has something even better in store. "More, please, babe."

Without a word, I feel the tip of his cock at my entrance. He's over me, supporting his weight with his arms while he rocks his erection against my pussy. Without the condom, the feel of his bare skin against me is more than I can take.

I suck in air and cry out, the need for him so deep, so consuming, that I slam my palms against his ass cheeks and practically drive him into me.

"You're so greedy, baby," he pants. "Tell me how bad you want me."

"Fuck," I hiss when he slips the tip of his cock just barely inside me. "Benny, please. Oh my God, please."

Instead of giving me what I want, he teases me, rocking his hips back and pulling his cock from my body, then nudging oh-so slightly forward.

"Benny," I cry, thrashing against the sheets, my knees open wide and my eyes slammed shut. "Benny, fuck me."

But he doesn't. Instead, he flips me onto my stomach and yanks my hips into the air. Then he kneels behind me and spreads my ass cheeks with his hands.

"I never want this to be over," he breathes, and I can't stop and analyze what he means.

I just need to feel it.

The mind-shattering bliss when his erection finally slides between my legs and into my body.

"Oh God." My face smashes into the mattress, my ass as high in the air as it can reach. "Deeper, deeper."

He obliges, but this isn't a hard fuck. This is a slow, deep coupling, his strokes long, his sighs that end in my name breathless and heady. He grips my hips like he's holding on to me for dear life, just like I'm gripping the blankets. I press back to meet his gentle thrusts, my need for release so intense that I'm bouncing, rocking, thrusting back against him, practically forcing him to fuck me harder.

This union, his bare skin against mine, this intimacy, is more than I've shared with anyone in a long, long time. It's so good. His length inside me, the pace of his thrusts, the pressure of his fingers.

The pleasure as he hits deep is so intense, I feel tears gather at the corners of my eyes.

"Touch yourself," he pants. "I want to feel you make yourself come."

Even though my face is down and my ass is up, I practically drag a weak hand between my legs. I don't need to touch myself, but I do, pressing two fingers against my clit while Benny picks up speed, thrusting harder, spurred on my throaty, desperate moans. My fingers slip along the front of my body, Benny fucking me harder from behind until, finally, I feel his cock get even larger and he slows, croaking out a helpless "Willow…" as he starts to come, and that sets me off.

I see nothing but darkness behind my lids, my face off the side so I can gasp in chestfuls of air as I come, wave after wave of pleasure flooding my body until I'm so weak, so done, my knees give out, and I collapse onto the bed.

Benny uses his arms to brace himself, lowering his body, his cock still inside me, until he's lying on top of me. I can feel the erratic pounding of his heartbeat against my back. My pussy throbs and my chest is squished under his weight. It's all so good. It's so much. His heat, his size, his perfection.

I giggle, forgetting that we didn't have the condom to hold back the mess.

But Benny doesn't seem to care. In fact, he pulls me closer, cuddling my face against his chest and tightening his arms around me.

I lie there quietly, my body cooling, my breaths perfectly in time with his. It's so much. The way he feels. The way I feel when I'm with him. It's amazing and arousing and exciting, but it's a lot. More than I've felt with anyone. Not just the sex, but this part. The way he holds me after. The way he dozes but still kisses me, my name a whisper on his lips, even when I think he's asleep.

This man is a lot. He might even be too much.

He's snoring lightly, his arms locked around me. But I can't sleep. I'm thinking, my mind whirling. "I'm going to get a sip of water," I whisper, kissing him lightly on the cheek.

He rolls over, tucking himself deep in the bedding.

I grab his T-shirt from the floor and toss it over my head, then head into the bathroom to clean up. Benny is still sleeping, so I head out to the kitchen and pour myself a glass of water. It's quiet, and the water of the river sparkles under the light of the moon.

I like it here. I've liked a lot of places I've lived. I've had some gorgeous homes, condos, yards, but I never expected to find a condo in a small town overlooking the river that would feel like home. Home isn't something I've had much of in my life. It's a strange feeling and not entirely unwelcome.

I check my phone for messages. I have three texts from Jessa, all venting about bloating and where exactly her newest show went off the rails.

I check my work email and have about twenty. Nothing pressing. I snooze them all until morning, until I reach one from a name I recognize.

Maggie Tempestini.

I click open the email and read it twice. I'm not sure I'm believing what I'm seeing, but I can only read it so many times before I know it's true.

Mags has sent me her résumé and a cover letter. She's applying for a job.

She wants to leave Benito.

CHAPTER 13
BENITO

A LOT HAS CHANGED over the last few weeks, and it's all Willow's fault. I can't get enough of the woman. She consumes my thoughts. When she sends me a text message during the day, my palms get sweaty, my heart starts racing, and a stupid grin eats up my face like I'm fourteen freaking years old.

The fact that I've been with her now for six weeks, almost seven, and I still feel as excited to see her every night as I did when we first met is surprising.

Things have changed slowly. We still fuck like horny teenagers, but we talk about everything. Her childhood, mine. The restaurant. Her business. Our friends and family. I know this thing, whatever it is we're doing, has an expiration date. She's leaving in a year, and I know that. But fuck if I don't want to stop time and stay here.

I've never felt this way about another woman before. I'm the short-time guy. Hook up and move on. That's what I've always done. And this should be the same thing.

But I can feel everything changing.

The only thing that hasn't changed is the shit with Mags. She's still avoiding me. After she called out of work without speaking to me, I took Willow's advice.

I asked Mags if we could talk, and we did. That went over like a week-old loaf of Italian bread. She stared at me, arms crossed, frowning while she said nothing was going on. She's fine. Everything's fine. She wasn't feeling well, apparently. She didn't apologize, didn't explain. Just listened, nodded, and repeated that line, "There's nothing to talk about. Everything's fine."

So, I've tried to act like everything is fine. Meanwhile, the application has been sitting on my desk staring me in the face. Although I can also feel the daggers as Mags glares into my back when we're in the kitchen together. I still need a roof. My office is a mess and worse than it's ever been. Because now, instead of working late or spending mornings in the office, I spend every spare moment I can with Willow.

I've been wanting to introduce her to my family, but I don't know. She's important to me. In ways I don't think I even fully understand. But how? What would I say? Hey, Ma, Pops, this is Willow...the woman I'm hooking up with until she moves away in a couple months.

The idea depresses me so much, I try to put it out of my head. But it's always there, like the scent of herbs in my kitchen, the pull of the heat and the drama and the pace of my business.

I am looking down at the SBA grant application that's due today. I sigh deeply. I know Willow has told me she's not the final decision-maker, but it doesn't make it any easier. Something about submitting this and asking for money that comes from her company.

None of it sits right with me.

I check the time. It's three in the afternoon. Mags is in the dining room, working on the schedule for next month. We've been hired to cater a rehearsal dinner at a venue off-site, so we are going to need to hire temporary staff to keep the restaurant functioning while we handle the event.

I wander out to the bar where Sassy is sitting at a table drinking a Coke that's mostly ice while she chatters with Mags. I nod at the few customers we have, then motion to an empty chair at the table.

"Mind if I crash the party?"

Sassy shakes her head, but Mags doesn't look up or even answer. I take a seat, and Sassy jumps up. "You want something, Benny?"

I shake my head but give my mom's friend and one of my best servers a smile. "Thanks, Sassy. I'm good."

She presses her lips together, then says, "My break's over. Later, Mags."

I frown and watch Sassy grab her glass and scurry off. I'm not one of those bosses who makes my employees punch a clock for every break. If it's slow and Sassy needs to have a seat, she knows I'm not going to care. Based on the way she hustled off, I have to assume that she and Mags were probably talking about me.

I motion toward the papers in front of Mags. "How's it look?" I ask.

She doesn't look up. "You know."

I rub my hands over my face. "No, actually. I don't. Care to go into a little more detail than that?"

She huffs a sigh, and my temper starts to flare. "The bride wants a three-course dinner with dessert and a salad course," she explains. "Appetizers during the cocktail hour, and then she does not want a buffet, but plated meals for three hundred guests. We are going to need a staff of at least six chefs. And the venue won't give us access because there is another event that morning until like four hours before service is scheduled to start. We're going to need staff here and at the venue to do prep, and then it's going to be tight."

I shake my head. I don't even need to look at the books to know we can't spare that kind of staffing. For a Saturday night, I'm going to need to hire and train people, but I may need a catering van to move food from here to the venue. I rub my eyes.

"What did we quote them per plate?"

She glares at me. "You gave them a discount. Remember?"

We don't cater a lot of off-site events, but this wedding is for one of my brother Franco's friends. I tried to cut him a good deal. I can see I cut deep into my profits in the process.

"Right," I sigh. "Okay, so what are our options? I can't hire six chefs, and unless I close Benito's for the night…"

She tosses her pencil on the table dramatically. Thankfully, there are no customers close to us, but Jas is behind the bar and she's staring at Mags with her mouth open.

"What's the problem?" I ask.

"You want me to work a fucking miracle, Benny, but I can't do this." She looks up, and her cheeks are red, her eyes glassy like she's near tears. "I know you don't like letting anyone near your books, but I don't know what we can afford or what we can't. We need six people minimum to manage this wedding, or we need to close the restaurant. I don't know what else you want me to do."

I stand up from the table, nearly tempted to grab the papers from her and throw them right in her face. But I'm the boss. It's my name on the front of the restaurant. Instead, I point to the papers and jerk a thumb toward my office.

"My office," I seethe. "Now."

I turn and storm away, Mags close on my heels.

Once we're in my office, I can't help myself. I slam the door and start yelling. "What the fuck, Mags?"

She yells right back at me. "Fuck what, Benny?"

I take a moment, compose my thoughts, and stomp toward my desk. "Mags," I say. "I don't know what's gotten under your skin. But I'm not going to accept 'It's fine' for an answer. What is wrong, and what can I do to get us back on track?"

Mags paces the far side of my office, looking stressed and angry. "I haven't been happy here for a long time, Benny."

This is news to me.

But I don't interrupt. I listen.

"When you hired me, I was so proud to work here. So proud. Benito Bianchi, king of Italian cuisine, saw something in me." The way she's saying it, it does not sound like a compliment.

Though my blood is boiling, I stay silent.

"But no matter what I do, you never take me seriously. There's no room to grow, Benny. You don't grow. You don't change." She waves a hand around accusingly. "This place has the same shitty carpeting you had when you hired me. Six years, Benny. Do you know how many times the carpet should be changed in a business like this? With the traffic we get, we should be doing updates constantly. Improvements, repairs."

Now that she's started, she's on a roll. "We have the same menu, the same vendors. The same servers." She gestures angrily toward the door. "Do you realize Rita is like eight hundred years old? Half the time, she can't hear the customers when they ask for a high chair or to be seated on the patio. And Sassy—"

I hold up a hand, trying hard as fuck to keep my hand from shaking. She has no right to talk about my staff, their age, or their performance. None. "Maggie, this is not about Sassy or Rita. I need to ask you to leave the team out of this. Just tell me about *you*."

She points at the grant application on the desk. "We need a new roof. You won't let me help with the books. You don't take any of my ideas seriously, so I don't even know why I'm here."

I draw in a deep breath through my nose. This conversation is going to be real fucking hard to come back from. I've broken up with a lot of women and have been dumped by many more. I can see the writing on the wall. So, I know I need to tread carefully. "So why are you still here, Mags." It's not a question, and I say it as calmly as I can.

Her lower lip trembles as she admits, "Because you're the best. Everybody knows it. I can't apply to work anywhere else because everyone in town is going to ask why the hell I would leave Benito's. I'm stuck." Her voice rises, but then she seems to realize she's close to shouting and calms down. "I'm stuck here with you, and you don't give two shits about the things that are important to me. You don't give two shits about me. So, what? I'm supposed to rot here until I'm Rita's age because there's no place else to go?"

I take a few deep breaths and remind myself that this is not a lover's quarrel. Mags and I have never so much as hugged a little too long. This is about work, and I need to keep my cool. No matter how my ego and my anger are firing at a rolling boil.

"Mags, I'm going to say a few things, and I'd like you to sit so I can say them to your face, not your back." I motion to a chair in front of my desk. "But if you don't want to sit, I'm not going to beg."

She crosses her arms over her chest and looks at me, a sad, hurt frown on her face. But then, as if she realizes she's backed me into a corner, she nods and drops into a chair. "Yeah," she says, brushing the hair back from her face. "Okay. Go ahead."

I choose my words very, very carefully. "Mags, you and I have worked together a long time. And I understand that you feel some attachment to this place. I rely on you like a business partner even though you're not. I'm sorry for that. I'm sorry if I created an expectation in you that you would have more authority over this place. I don't know how we got here, but here's where we're going."

I meet her eyes, my stare cold but kind. At least, I hope it is. "Hear me on this, because I'm not fucking around. This is my business. My place. Everything from the shit carpeting to the employees you may think you're better than."

She opens her mouth to interrupt me, but I hold up a hand. "Please," I say firmly. "Let me finish. I'll let you have your say, but I need to get this out."

She swallows hard and leans back in the chair, arms still tight over her chest.

"You are a tremendous asset in the kitchen, and that's what you're paid to be. Nothing more, nothing less. You do work for the best fucking restaurant in Star Falls, and that means not only me but that means everyone else I choose to have as part of this operation. I will not—do you understand me on this?—will not stand by while you insult the team that stands by me day after day."

What I don't say is that these people are family to me. I'd sooner shoot off my own foot than fire Rita. The day I tell Sassy she has to go because she's old is the day I shut the doors on this place for good.

I may not be the best businessman, but I know my values. Food, people, and customers.

Those are what matter and in that order.

"Now," I tell her, "I appreciate that you've taken the initiative to complete this application, but I'm not going to submit it." Her eyes widen, but I push on. "I'm not going to apply for the SBA grant. You don't have to like it, you don't have to agree with it, but it's my decision. End of discussion."

Mags looks down at her clogs, her lips pinched in a tight frown.

"We've had our differences, and I'm going to say one more thing, and then I'm going to let you speak." I take a deep breath and lean over my desk toward her. "Mags, as much as you've meant to me all these years, I can't have the attitude you've shown around here. Not toward me, and certainly not toward your team. Now, I'd like you to tell me what you plan to do. I need to be surrounded by people who have my back. Not the other way around. I'm not going to watch my back in my own restaurant. If you can't stay, then I'll give you a great reference. It's that simple."

I clamp my lips together, congratulating myself on keeping my fucking cool.

Mags meets my eyes. "I've been applying," she says quietly. "I wanted you to send in that grant because I applied for a job with Culinary Creations. I sent Willow my résumé a couple weeks ago. I was hoping if she saw the application, she'd know what a great job I did pulling it together and would interview me."

I congratulated myself way too soon. "Excuse me?" I seethe. "You did what?"

She lifts her chin. "I sent Willow my résumé. I was hoping to get in on the ground of the new place. Make a name for myself."

I feel my guts stir around in my belly, and a sour flavor coats my tongue. "What'd she say? Was she happy to poach my best employee right out from under me?"

Mags shakes her head. "She was kind of weird about it. That's why I've been so stressed out. If I fucked up by reaching out to her and I fucked over things with you…" She laughs, a bitter, grating sound.

"What do you mean, she was weird about it?" I ask. I can't deny that I'm curious. "What did she say?"

Mags lifts a shoulder and shrugs. "She just talked about what a great guy you are, such a good cook and a good man." She flicks a look at me. "She talks about you like she knows you. Like she's in love with you or something. But she said she's not interviewing now and that I should communicate with you. Give you a chance to work through any issues we're having."

My heart swells at Mags's words.

We're both quiet for a second. The reality of what we've said, what's left unsaid, and what can't be unsaid hangs between us.

"Where does that leave things?" I finally ask her. "I'd like to resolve this so I know whether I need to replace you."

"I'd like to take some time off," Mags says. "I have a couple vacation days left. A week, I think."

I nod. "Okay."

"Can you cover the kitchen?" Mags looks worried, sucking her lower lip between her teeth.

"Absolutely. You take the time you need. I'll handle the rest," I assure her.

Mags stands and walks toward the door. I don't know what the right thing to do now is. Do I thank her?

Give her a stern warning? I've never fired anyone. This is as close as I've gotten. I've always had Mags to do the tough stuff for me.

"Hey, Mags," I say, stopping her before she can leave.

She looks back at me, the expression on her face as uncertain as I feel.

"I appreciate everything you've done over the years. Don't think a day goes by that I'm not crystal fucking clear how much weight you carry here. Thank you. No matter what happens from here, thank you."

She blinks fast, nods once, then leaves.

I look over the grant application on my desk, then crumple it in my hands, tear it in two, and toss it in the trash bin. Then I grab my phone.

Me: You got some time? I'd like to talk to you about some things.

Willow replies a minute later.

Willow: I'm in the city for a last-minute meeting with a contractor. I might not be home until late. Tomorrow? We could spend the morning together...

Me: Morning, yes. Will I see you tonight when you're back?

There's a long pause before Willow responds. I hold the phone in my hands, shocked at the way my heartbeat picks up and my breath tightens in my chest as I wait. We've spent every night together for almost two months now. Why would tonight be any different?

But then the message comes.

Willow: B, I need to handle some stuff tonight. Text me in the morning?

I'm stunned at how disappointed I am.

Is Willow seeing someone else?

Why else would she need a night to herself?

I consider asking her, but look where that got me with Mags. Demanding answers and confrontation might just lead to shit I'm not ready to handle.

I thumbs-up the text and don't say more. I put the phone in my desk drawer and drop my face into my hands. I'm probably losing Mags. I may be losing Willow even sooner than I expected.

Somehow with just two conversations, this shitshow that is my life got even shittier.

CHAPTER 14
WILLOW

I MAKE the drive back to Star Falls after dark, listening to nothing but the sounds of the road under my tires and the racing of my own thoughts.

The season has changed in the time I've been here. Early fall has shifted from colorful and brilliant, the bright green grass softening to a sleepy color, the bold red and orange leaves long swept into piles, the trees having dropped most of their leaves.

All day, I've felt hollow, and I can't figure out why.

The Kincade family's attorney sent the demand letter as promised. The people who came to my company wanting to open a second location are now completely done. They essentially are insisting that if we don't release them from the contract, they will file an injunction to stop the progress on the new location. They intend to file a lawsuit to try to terminate the contract altogether.

There was no demand made. No explanation that

they want more money or more creative control. Nothing. They didn't even explain what the basis of the lawsuit would be.

Theresa hasn't said anything yet, but I know what this means—I'll be pulled back from Star Falls. Right now, there is no other deal ready for me to move to, so I'll likely live here or from a suitcase while I hit the road, looking for another destination.

Normally, the idea of getting back on the road excites me. After a year on a project, the thrill of a new place makes me feel alive. I love adventure. I'm curious and, to be honest, a little restless. I am usually the one chomping at the bit to say goodbye to the old and a hearty hello to the new.

But today, none of my typical enthusiasm is anywhere to be found. I think about the cities I might explore, the cuisines just waiting to develop into viable businesses. Instead of curious or even just ready, I feel deflated.

I sigh as my eyes adjust to the familiar streets that lead to my condo. The place I've called home—if only temporarily. The place where I've cooked and laughed, taken calls for work, and video-chatted with Jessa.

The place where I first received flowers from Benny.

The place where I look forward to seeing him every single night.

Benito Bianchi.

It's really him, I think, that I will miss the most. What started out as just a hookup, a short-term whatever this is… I don't know.

I'm starting to think that what bothers me most about leaving Star Falls is the thought of leaving Benny.

Which, honestly, doesn't make any sense.

This will be the first project I've been pulled off prematurely. I have no condo back in Chicago. No storage unit full of memories where I can wander through the past, no aunt or cousins to crash with while I figure out my next move.

My childhood was a nightmare. Parents who were more enamored with alcohol than they were with me. My mom stayed with my dad much longer than she should have until, finally, he left her in the worst way possible. He died in a car accident. The irony of it was that my dad wasn't even intoxicated at the time. He swerved to avoid hitting a deer, blew a tire, and hit a tree.

Once my mother lost my dad, she descended quickly into more drinking. By the time I was in high school, Mom was in active kidney failure, on dialysis, and battling late-stage lung cancer. There was no extended family to take me in, so I spent the last year of high school in a foster home. The people who cared for me were nice enough. I was fed. I had an allowance and decent clothes. I wasn't mistreated. But I was basically a stranger living under a roof with people I didn't know. Who didn't really want me there. They were not bad to me. And that's the best I can say about them.

At least they were an improvement in some ways over my own parents.

During that year in foster care is when I developed the one-year rule. I promised myself that I could survive anything for just one year. And if I did, I'd never have another bad year in my life. I'd travel, meet amazing people, do cool things. And I have.

I've been on my own ever since I turned eighteen, and I have lived every day the way I wanted to. Making great money. Eating great food. I travel. I have a gorgeous wardrobe. I have enough of what I want to feel happy, but not so much that I can't pick up and move when the spirit and timing move me. I am a pro at adulthood. I know how to keep people I love close and leave anything that doesn't make me happy behind.

By every definition that I've ever cared about, I should be blissfully happy.

But now, facing the disruption of what should have been another easy year, I'm feeling conflicted.

No, worse than that—I'm miserable.

When I reach home, I see that Benny's parking spot is empty. He must still be at the restaurant. I'm suddenly gripped by an idea. I should go there. Get my ass back in the car and go there now just to see him. I don't know what I was thinking, telling him I needed a night to myself. I met with a roofing contractor in Cleveland this afternoon, and I didn't want Benny to know the whole truth yet.

The fact that I'm leaving. I don't see how I'm going to see Benny and not tell him the truth. I know what's coming, and I don't know that once I see him, I'll be able to keep it from him.

I lock my car and grab my purse, stopping myself from running to him. I go into my unit, call Jessa, and then take a long, hot bath. I put on my comfiest pajamas. I climb onto the couch and look out through the windows at the view of the river. Something tightens in my chest. I've grown so attached to this place and to the fact that he's just on the other side of that wall.

I get up and grab my phone from the counter to check the time. It's almost ten, which means Benny should be home any time now if he's closing up the restaurant. If he didn't, he's probably already next door.

I type in a text and hit send before I can talk myself out of it.

Me: I'm home, and I would love to see you if you're up for it. Rough day. Fair warning, I might not be good company.

I climb on the couch and turn on the TV. I flip through the channels but can't settle on anything that will hold my interest. All I can think about is the fact that I might be leaving. I am leaving. The words vibrate in my head until my temples throb. I want to clutch the arms of my couch and slow down time, but I can't.

I don't hear back from Benny, and after thirty minutes, my stomach starts to hurt. I'm such a fool. When I told him I was busy, he probably called someone else. He had a whole life before we started hooking up. He's probably with someone else right now.

Earlier today when I said I needed space, I practically gave him my blessing to go there. I told him I needed alone time, and now I'm telling him I want him. What a freaking mess.

I turn off the TV and decide to try to sleep, when there is a soft knock at my door. My head jerks up, and my pulse starts racing. I rush to the door, check the peephole, and when I see the familiar dark stubble and dimpled chin, I throw open the lock.

I don't say anything, just stand there staring. Benny looks like he's been hit by a truck. There are bags under his eyes, and the corners of his lips pull down into a slight frown.

"Rough day?" he asks, pointing to me. Then he points to himself. "Total shit day."

He opens his arms, and I go to him, resting my head against his chest and holding him so tight, I can't believe he can breathe.

"Come on," he says. "Let's go to bed."

He comes inside, and I lock the door. He strips off his shoes and coat, then follows me wordlessly to my room. He peels off all his clothes except his boxer briefs, and we climb under the covers. For the first time ever, we don't fuck like bunnies. We don't laugh, kiss, or even grind against each other. He rolls onto his side, tucks me close against him, and strokes my hair. We stay awake like that for what feels like hours. No talking. Only him holding me and breathing into my hair.

When my arms start to fall asleep, we roll over, again without a word, and this time, I spoon him. I press my cheek against the hot muscles of his back, an arm thrown over his body. I bury my face against his skin and just breathe him in. It's so quiet, so still. I hear the soft sounds of his breathing, the steady beat of his heart in time with mine, and tears inexplicably burn my eyes.

This is so good. It's so good in so many ways. I don't know if he feels it too, but it's the most poignant and painful goodbye.

The somber mood follows us into the next morning. I wake before Benny and get up to use the bathroom. When I come back to bed, he's lying on his back, his eyes open.

"You still want to spend the day together?" His voice is thick with emotion.

"Yes," I tell him. "I'll start some coffee."

"Come back to bed first?" He sits up, and I climb in beside him. He opens his arms, and I slip under the blankets.

The sheets are warm and wrinkled, and I just want to snuggle down with him and never, ever leave.

The thought hits me, and I realize it's true.

I don't want to leave. Not Star Falls. Not this condo. Even more than that, I don't want to leave him.

I close my eyes as he strokes my hair and murmurs a question. "Were you going to tell me that Mags sent you her résumé?" he asks.

My eyes fly open, and I look up at him. "No," I say sincerely. "Benny, I would not have told you. Her career goals and job search are her private business. I wouldn't have gotten involved in whatever business you two need to sort out. But I also had no intention of hiring her. I wouldn't steal your most valuable employee from you."

"Not stealing." He wraps his arms around me, and I reluctantly settle back against his chest. "It's not stealing if she wants to leave, Willow." He doesn't sound angry, only resigned. "I'm hurt. Angry, maybe. She told me she sent her résumé over to you. I guess she even filled out the grant application partly to impress you with her skills."

I sigh. "So, she talked to you? Was that yesterday? Your shit day?"

"We talked, all right." He sounds so subdued. Defeated. Sort of like how I feel. "I wouldn't blame you if you did want to hire her," he tells me. "She's been amazing for the last six years. But lately, things have been rough. I wouldn't hold that against her, though. Things end, and not usually great things. I'd give her a good reference. I'll do it right now if you want."

I again pull out of his hold and shake my head. "Benny, I don't want to hire Mags."

I don't want to admit to him that I can't. I won't have a restaurant at all—no staff, no kitchen, no contractors. Everything I have worked for is about to go up in smoke. But I am not ready to talk about it. Not until it's official. Maybe there's a tiny part of me holding out some hope that there is some other way.

"But," I tell him, "if I did have an interest in hiring her, I would talk to you about it before I made a move."

I meet his eyes, and I know he believes me. His shoulders soften and he nods. "Come on," he says. "Let's shower. I have a plan for us."

"A plan?" We didn't make plans, other than to spend the day together. "What kind of plan?"

He kisses me softly. "You'll see. You up for a little adventure today?"

I sigh into his kiss and nod. "Yeah, I am."

While I make coffee and shower, Benny goes home, showers, and gets dressed. I email Alex and Theresa that

I'm going to be out of the office handling some personal business until early afternoon, but that I'll be available this afternoon. I assume Benny has to work later, and thankfully, I don't have any meetings or emails that can't wait until later.

Once he's back, we eat a quiet breakfast, the strain of our separate stresses keeping us both quiet. After we eat, he tells me to wear comfy shoes and a warm coat, so I dress for the late November weather, and we head out.

"So," I ask as he pulls out of the parking garage. "What are we doing?"

He reaches across the center console and takes my hand. "A little tour of Star Falls. You've mostly seen the inside of my bedroom, but I'd like to show you some more of the fine small town you're going to call home for at least the next few months."

My stomach churns, the delicious breakfast and coffee not at all happy with this plan. "Benny, I…" But I don't know what to say. If I tell him that I'm leaving, that Star Falls won't be my home, then what? We go back to my place and break up now?

I don't want that. In fact, I don't want that even more than I don't want to take a tour of Star Falls. So instead, I lace my fingers tightly through his. "I'd like that," I say.

At least what I'm saying is the truth, even if it's not the whole truth.

We drive through a lovely-looking neighborhood. The houses are on the small side, a mixture of brick and siding. But they are, for the most part, comfortable and well-maintained, only a few here and there showing signs of neglect and wear. Even though fall has blown the leaves from the trees and most of the flowering plants have gone dormant, the neighborhood feels safe and homey.

There are minivans and pickup trucks parked on the street, and most of the homes don't have fences. I see plenty of swing sets and above-ground backyard pools. This is definitely a place where people raise families. Host holidays. I wonder how crowded the streets are with bikes and baby strollers in the summer.

Finally, Benny pulls to a stop and parks the SUV on the street.

"Where are we?" I ask.

He turns to me, the hint of a smile finally warming his face. "This is my childhood home. Where I grew up."

I cock my chin at him in confusion. "Your childhood home? Your parents' house? Are they home?"

He shrugs. "Possibly. I don't know. Maybe. It's early, so probably."

I narrow my eyes at him. "Benny, are you trying to introduce me to your parents? Is that…"

I stop myself because it can't be.

First of all, I'm wearing yoga pants and running shoes. My hair is in a bun. I don't have cookies or wine or flowers. I mean, it's been years since I met anyone's parents in a dating-type situation. I don't date like most people. I don't stick around long enough for most guys I hook up with to want this.

I'm not sure how I feel about it.

"Benny, I don't think this is a good idea."

He nods, looking immediately hurt. Something sharp flashes across his face. "Yeah, I'm sorry. I thought maybe it'd be a bad idea. Never mind. It's okay." He looks away from me, suddenly withdrawing. I feel like he's pulled into himself and disappeared, and the feeling fucking guts me. He puts both hands on the wheel and turns on the ignition.

"No," I say. "That's not what I mean."

I reach out and hold his arm firmly.

"Turn off the truck. I want to meet your parents. I would have liked to dress a little nicer, and I would have brought them something. Flowers, cookies, I don't know."

He turns his head slightly, his warm brown eyes searching my face. "It's okay. I probably fucked this up. I should have asked you. I should have…" He groans. "Willow, I've been fucking up everything in my life lately."

I don't know what Benny's been going through. The stress with Mags might just be a part of it. We've spent so much time having fun, having sex, and talking about surface-issue stuff that I can see there are ways he might need something more than that. He needs a girlfriend. A relationship. I can't be that for him. I won't be staying, but I can do this. I can meet his parents. If it brings him one ounce of peace today, I can get through it.

"Come on," I say, opening the door and jumping to

the curb. "You promised me a tour. There's no better place to start than here."

He climbs out of the SUV, clicks the locks, then holds my hand as we walk up to the front door. The air around us is heavy. This feels important. I'm meeting his parents. The guy I've been hooking up with for two months.

Am I his girlfriend?

What will he say to them?

I don't have a ton of time to wonder because he unlocks the door with a key and holds open the screen for me.

"Shoes off, if you don't mind," he says, removing his boots once we're in the front hallway.

I slip out of my runners and hand him my jacket, which he hangs on a hook by the door. Then, we walk inside.

The Bianchi family home is dark, like maybe his parents are still asleep, but Benny doesn't seem too worried.

"Ma. Pops," he calls out, motioning for me to follow him. The second we walk into the living room, I see Benny's demeanor change completely.

He's smiling, and his whole body seems to relax. The gorgeous brooding brown eyes go soft, crinkling at the corners. He runs a hand through his hair and smiles at me. Beaming. He's happy, and he seems very happy that I'm here too.

This is what it looks like to go home. This is what home feels like.

A wave of longing, disappointment, and regret

washes over me. I'm suddenly certain this is a terrible idea.

My knees buckle, and I brace myself. Benny knows that I lost my parents and spent a year in foster care. But we've only talked about the easy stuff. The fact that my foster family was used to younger kids, so my bedroom for my entire senior year of high school was Barbie-pink and filled with dolls. He knows I taught myself to cook that year because my foster parents both worked and hated cooking.

My parents had never been great at consistency, so I had always had an interest in cooking. But spending hours alone after school in my foster parents' kitchen is where I fell in love with food. I could chop, read recipes, and tweak them based on things I knew I preferred. That year was life-changing in good ways, but what I never shared was how lonely it was. How I felt closer to YouTube cooking show hosts and social media chefs than I did anyone in my life.

Food has always meant home to me, not any one place. Family has been the friends I choose, not any one person or group of people.

But walking through Benny's parents' house, I can see into the life that formed this man. Framed pictures of Benito and his siblings hang on the walls and cover end tables. Artwork scribbled by the Bianchis' grandkids wallpapers the entire fridge. Benny walks through the first floor, petting two dogs who both look too old to bark at me, a stranger who no doubt smells like Benny.

He heads toward the back of the house and flips on

the kitchen lights. "You want something to drink?" he asks. "Glass of water?"

I shake my head. It's surreal walking through the quiet space. The dining room table is exactly what I'd expect. A long table has a couple of leaves that extend the length to fit the twelve chairs that surround it. A table runner goes down the middle, and a basket of fresh oranges and apples sits in the center.

Benny fills a glass of water and motions for me to sit at the table. I take a seat, and immediately, my mind fills with images of the many years that he has eaten meals here. Spent time with his parents, his sister and brothers. A longing and a sense of loss hit me so hard, it's as if someone has stolen the air from my lungs.

"This okay?" he asks, smoothing my hair back from my face. He's standing beside me, sipping a glass of water.

I'm not okay, but I nod. "Are they home?" I ask. Maybe they're out. Maybe this is just a tiny little baby step into Benny's world. Maybe we'll leave and I'll never have to put all the pieces together. I'll never have to see all that I've missed out on in my life right here in front of my eyes. I won't actually have to meet the people who make this house a home.

Benny nods. "Ma's probably sewing upstairs. I'll go check if they don't come down in a minute."

As if they're summoned by Benny's words, we hear feet on the stairs.

"I'll be right back, honey." A man's voice, gravelly and warm and sounding a lot like Benny's, echoes through the house.

We both turn toward the voice, and I feel Benny's hand tighten on my shoulder. "That's my pops," he says softly, his voice brimming with love and pride.

I stand from the chair, and Benny tucks me under his arm. For a moment, I feel like a kid again, like we're going to prom or something and he's excited to show off his date to his parents. I plaster a grin on my face, hoping I don't look terrified. But that grin melts into a mask of horror when I set eyes on the man coming toward the dining room.

The man has a full head of thick gray hair, its waves long like Benny's but disheveled. His chest is completely bare, and as my eyes roam down his body, I realize he's not just shirtless. He's butt-ass naked. Nude. I'm talking not a stitch of clothes from his head to his bare feet. And he's sporting a massive erection that bobs ominously with every step he takes toward us.

"Jesus fucking Christ!" Benny shouts and turns me toward him, clamping a hand over my eyes. "Pops, what the fuck?"

"Benny?" Benny's dad says slowly, his voice disbelieving and low. But then, as if it hits him all at once, he starts cursing. "Oh shit. I'm sorry. Oh shit."

"Pops, for fuck's sake. Don't apologize. Go put on some goddamn pants."

"What's going on, Mario?" And that must be Benny's mom. I cover my eyes tight with my hands, lower my face into Benny's warm plaid shirt, and do my almighty best not to laugh.

Then, Benny's hand still clamped over my eyes, I hear a rush of footsteps, a lot of very loud voices talking over each other, and doors slamming. Only when Benny releases me do we look at each other, our eyes wide with shock.

Then we double over, breathless with agonizing, uncontrolled, gut-wrenching laughter.

CHAPTER 15
BENITO

MY PARENTS SIT beside each other at the dining room table, holding hands. My mother's face is beaming, her cheeks flaming red. Thank the sweet Lord almighty Ma is dressed, and Pops is not only covered from head to toe in clothing, but he's also wearing his glasses. I wouldn't mind a hood, a bucket, or an eye mask for myself. Anything to protect my eyes from any more unexpected *sights*.

"This is new for us, you see," Ma's explaining. She seems a little embarrassed but mostly happy. Wish I could say the same for myself. "We didn't know what to expect, and since I have the no-drinks-upstairs rule, your father had to come downstairs to get some water. And well…we thought we were alone."

I hold up a hand, feeling simultaneously queasy and like I might burst into nervous laughter all over again. "Ma, I don't want to know the details of whatever the hell that was that I walked in on. Could we just move past it and never, ever speak of it again? Except maybe in therapy. Because I'm scarred. Literally traumatized. All the good work you guys did raising me? Undone with one…" I wave my hand at Pops. "Just one look and decades of solid parenting down the drain."

"Now, son." Pops is looking at me over the rims of his glasses. "You know you're always welcome here, but when you stop in at eight o'clock in the morning…"

"Pops." I shake my head. "You have grandkids coming in and out all day. What if one of them were here?"

I'm not that mad, but I'm still weirded out. Reality-check time. My parents still have sex. Whoopee. Great for them. Am I okay with the idea that they still get it on? Yes, sure. But does that mean I want to see it happen? Did I ever, and I do mean literally ever, need to see my dad's dick let alone my dad sporting wood for my ma?

Abso-friggin-lutely not.

I think I'm going to be sick.

Ma gets up from the table and clasps my hand. "Honey," she says in a low voice. "This is what's been going on with your father."

"Just tell him, Lucia." Pops is shaking his head. "It's not like it's going to stay a secret." He points into his lap. "I don't know how long it'll be till this stuff wears off, but I'm not getting up from the table until it does."

"Stuff? Wears off? What the hell did you two do?" I grimace, trying to block out visions of sex lubes and toys and massage oils out of my mind.

I might actually vomit. I cough into my hand.

"Benny," Ma says, her voice soothing and sweet like

she's talking to a toddler and not her adult son. "Now that your father and I are empty nesters, we have been enjoying each other's company. We're like newlyweds again."

I hear the tiniest little huff of a giggle from Willow, and I groan, a full-body sound that comes with a massive grimace. Willow seems to be taking her unwilling role in my parents' sex life a little too well.

Talk about a memory that will last a lifetime. I can't believe she hasn't run screaming from the house already. I flick a glance her way, and her eyes are wide, her lips pressed together tight, either to hold back laughter or— if she's feeling like me—the puke that threatens to spew out if I don't get a grip.

"Ma, for fuck's sake, please…"

"Benny. Language." Ma's face, bare of makeup for once, looks stern. She looks over to Willow. "I'm sorry. You must think Benny was raised in a barn."

Willow shakes her head, those perfect lips still clamped shut. She manages to squeak out, "No, uh, not at all."

Ma looks back to me, her face brightening with happiness. "Benny, your father went to the *doctor* a while back," she puts such a strong emphasis on the word doctor that I immediately understand what she means. "He had some tests done to make sure he was in good health…"

"I got Viagra," he says bluntly, pointing down to his lap. "You just happened to walk in during our maiden voyage."

"Pops." I nearly scream it. I don't know how much more of this I can take, but then it hits me.

Ma's trying to tell me that Pops is okay. I look to her for assurance. "So, that was all about this?" I put my hand out palm up, and then I raise just my index finger nice and slow, to imitate a growing erection. "Everything is okay?"

"Everything is great," Ma assures me.

"I'm not so sure it's great." Pops frowns and fidgets in his seat. "Does anyone know how to turn this thing off?"

"Pops." I rub my face so hard I hope my eyes get ripped out of my head so I can't see my dad squirming around because his dick won't get soft.

I hear Willow giggle beside me. "Honestly," she says, "if having your son walk in on you doesn't do the job, I don't know what would."

I turn to Willow, and both my parents stare at her. Then, like someone clicked a switch, all four of us burst out into laughter. Ma slaps the table to hold up her weight, and my father looks like he's actually in pain, which he probably is.

Willow wipes tears from her red cheeks, she's laughing so hard, and I have to get up and pace the room because I give myself the hiccups from lack of air.

Finally, when we all calm down, Ma comes around the table and hugs Willow's shoulders. "Well, welcome to the family, Willow. After all this, I think you're officially a Bianchi."

By the time Pops's hard-on decides to make a graceful exit, it's nearly ten o'clock. Willow and Ma are upstairs looking at something Ma's sewing. I'm in the kitchen with my pops alone, thankful that he can stand and walk without having to follow his erection around.

"So, Pops," I say. "You had Ma worried as hell. Everything check out with the doctor?"

Mario nods. "Because of my age, my local doctor wanted some special heart tests. Then those people sent me to urology, and it just went on from there. Anybody and everybody got a look at my junk before they'd put me on any medicine to help in that department." Pops shrugs. "I guess it's a good thing, but I had more people with their hands down my pants than I did when I was single."

I groan, but Pops continues.

"Clean bill of health. A starter dose of some meds to help me in the bedroom, and we'll see if things improve. Although…" he looks at me, lifting a thick silver brow. "Nothing kills the mood quite like your son and his new girlfriend walking in on the fun. I may have to take a double dose next time."

"Please, God. Pops, can you not? I'm thrilled you're okay, but I never, ever want to get this close to your sex life again."

"You know, son, if it weren't for your mother and I having such a great time in the bedroom, we wouldn't have made four kids."

"Pops, I don't think *my* heart is healthy enough for this kind of stress." I shake my head and breathe a deep sigh of relief when he changes the subject.

"So, Willow…" he says. "It's been a long time since

you brought a woman home to your parents. Is it serious? I didn't even know you were seeing anyone."

I don't know how to answer his questions, but I do what I always do with my folks. I tell the truth. "She's amazing," I say, not able to stop a grin from covering my face. "She's brilliant and funny. I learned today she's incredibly resilient."

I glare at Pops, and he chuckles.

"We've known each other a couple months, but she's only in Star Falls a short time."

Pops's smile fades away. "How short?"

I shrug. "A year, tops."

Mario claps a hand on my shoulder. "I'm sorry. Where does she live full time?" he asks. "Would long-distance be an option?"

I shrug again. "There's a little more," I tell him. I explain the age gap. The fact that she doesn't want to have kids. That her business might put mine out of business.

"And yet, you brought her here," Pops says. "To meet us. She means something to you, Benny."

I nod. "I think so."

That's not the whole truth. I know so. I'm sure of it, actually. The more I talk about the reality of Willow leaving eventually, the more I know I can't let her go. I don't want her to leave me. Don't want her to leave Star Falls. I don't know what I need to do, but maybe, just maybe… I have under a year, but who knows. By that time, maybe I'll be able to convince her to stay.

My pops hugs me and holds me tight. "You deserve

happiness, Benny. And nothing really good ever comes without complications. You'll work it out."

He releases me, and I search my dad's face. "How can you be sure?" I ask. "There are so many things stacked against us. How can I be sure it's not all going to be too much?"

"Too much?" My pops echoes my words. "It's never too much. Not when you love someone," he assures me. "Just trust that, Benny. No obstacle you two might face will be too much. Not if you don't let it."

The front door opens, and my sister Gracie breezes in, her toddler on her hip. "Ma! Pops!" she shouts. "You guys busy?"

"Oh, they were," I mutter under my breath. "Sorry, but I had to say it."

Mario groans and sniffs in indignation. "Well, if a man can't make love to his wife in his own house…"

"Hold the phone." One of Gracie's thick brows is sky-high in her forehead, her lips pulled into a grossed-out grimace. "Did Pops just say he was *making love to his wife?*"

"Don't even get me started," I tell her, shaking my head. "I saw it, Gracie. Saw things no man should ever see."

Gracie puts the baby down, and he toddles over to me. I open my arms for a hug and murmur against his neck. "Make it go away, Ethan. Make the memory go away."

Grace looks horrified as she hugs Pops and holds up a hand. "Stop. I have already heard more than enough."

"Pops got himself on Viagra," I offer. I use my finger

to again simulate a hard-on, and Gracie makes a puking sound.

"Oh my God, I told you to stop." She smacks me on the arm. "That's sick."

"It's nature. It's natural, I mean…" Pops holds his hands in the air. "I give up. I'm sorry your brother had to see my morning wood, Gracie, but…"

"Pops. Oh my God, stop." Gracie covers her mouth like she might actually puke when Ma and Willow come down the stairs. Gracie turns to our mom and kisses her cheek. "Don't tell me," she says. "Ma, I don't have the stomach to hear about your sex life."

"Gracie, please, it's bad enough that Willow had to meet your father for the first time in the nude, but in front of the baby." My mother scowls. "Let's leave the bedroom talk to the grown-ups, please."

Gracie is covering her entire face with her hands. She's squeezing her eyes, heavily winged with eyeliner, closed, and she's making a fake-retching sound behind her hands. "Oh my fucking God, I'm leaving. I'm done."

"Language." Ma never misses even one curse.

Willow is standing behind my mom, grinning at me and watching the scene unfold. When Gracie finally uncovers her mouth, she looks from Willow to me and then back at Willow. "Please tell me you're with my brother and you have nothing to do with the apparent sex den my parents have turned this place into."

Willow extends a hand to Gracie. "I am with your brother. Willow Watkins."

Gracie looks at her hand but then says, "Are you not a hugger?"

Willow grins, a large smile that lights up her whole face. "No, no. Hugs are great."

Gracie clasps her in her arms, the neck of her very loose boatneck top falling over one shoulder, revealing both a bright-red bra strap and an arm loaded with ink. "Nice to meet you. I'm the smart one in the family, and this is my kid, Ethan. I have two more in school."

Willow nods and bends down to greet my nephew. While she's kneeling, Gracie spins and throws a look at me. "What's with all the secrets in this house? Ma and Pops have set up a sex dungeon, and you have a girlfriend? Do Vito and Franco know?"

"There is no sex dungeon," my father says on a long sigh. "And I don't know if your brothers know about Benny's girlfriend, but this is the first we're meeting her."

"And she is wonderful." Ma is beaming.

She hasn't even put on makeup yet, which means she's really feeling comfortable around Willow. Not that she has had any time since Willow and I interrupted her and Pops.

"She is wonderful, and Pops and Ma are healthy and *active*." I grimace as I emphasize active. "And Willow and I were just leaving." I nod at Willow, who is looking at my sister like she's about to burst out laughing.

"So soon? Can't you stay for lunch?" Ma picks up Ethan and smooches him loudly on the cheek.

"Ma, I might never get my appetite back." I lean down and kiss her goodbye, then give Ethan a loud raspberry on his chubby little neck. "I'm kidding. Love you, but we got places to be."

I give Pops a hug and am about to make a joke, when it hits me. My father's okay. He isn't hiding a health scare. He's not sick. He's doing pretty fucking great, actually. The reality fills my chest with relief, and I hold him for a long time. "I'm so grateful you're all right, Pops," I say, my voice low. "I just wish I didn't learn you were okay by seeing your dick out."

I pound Pops on the back, and he laughs again, seemingly unfazed by how scarred I am. He puts a hand on my shoulder and meets my eyes. "I will never leave my bedroom naked and aroused again, son."

"Oh my God, Pops." Gracie fake-retches again, and now I know Pops is enjoying this.

Ma brings Willow into a three-way hug, balancing Ethan on one hip and squeezing her tight. "You come back Sunday for dinner," she tells Willow. "Even if Benny is working and can't be here. Our home is always open to you. And if you don't have plans for Thanksgiving, you're invited. And Christmas. We don't usually do a big meal for New Year's Eve because the kids like to go out or do their own thing, but you are always welcome."

I swoop in and tug on Willow's hand. "Let's say goodbye to Pops before Ma gives you a house key and invites you to little Ethan's high school graduation in about sixteen years."

"Would that be such a bad thing?" Ma asks.

My pops gives Willow a quick hug, and I hear him

apologize again. Whatever he says has her flushing with real laughter.

"I won't, I promise," she says.

We walk hand in hand toward the front door, put on our shoes, and then stop because Gracie meets us at the door.

"Bye, asshole," she says, giving me a "what the fuck are you doing" voice. "What am I? Chopped liver? No goodbye for your sister?"

I kiss my sister's cheek, and Willow gives Gracie another hug. As we're walking out the door, I call behind me, "Ma, Pops, make sure y'all are careful. We don't need any more siblings."

Willow and I run to my car as they assault us with laughs and the sounds of Grace's fake retching.

CHAPTER 16
WILLOW

"SOOOO," I say as Benny navigates the SUV away from the curb. "Your parents seem nice."

Benny looks at me and then widens his eyes. He's got both hands gripping the wheel, and I can tell he's seriously shaken by what we just saw. "Lemme tell you," he says. "They are the best people ever. But that…" He clears his throat. "That was way too much for a first meeting."

Way too much.

A first meeting.

It was a lot, but Benny's parents are everything I would have expected. And more than anyone could ever ask for. Warm, loving, and welcoming. I felt immediately at home in their house, and worse, I didn't want to leave.

"If this is what your parents pull out on a first meeting, I'm not sure I can handle Thanksgiving and Christmas," I tell him, something low in my belly gnawing at me. A part of me desperately wishes I'd still be here for either of those holidays. Was there a part of me that had already picked out the corner of the condo right near the windows where I'd set up a tree?

I feel like the last two months have been a fever dream of sex and pretty lies. But I'm sure now that the pretty lies had nothing to do with Benny and everything to do with me. How I feel about never staying in one place for very long. How I feel about fresh starts and new adventures. How can I love something so much and grow tired of it at the same time?

I try to add a smile after my words because the truth is unfolding inside my heart faster than I can stop it, and I feel like I might cry. As we pull away from his parents' house, I'm really conflicted about leaving.

"Where to now?" I ask, trying to sound bright. If Benny has to work this afternoon, we only have a couple more hours together. I want to enjoy every last minute.

"You'll see." He tightens his fingers through mine but doesn't meet my eyes. He stares straight ahead at the road as he tells me about his family.

By the time I realize where we are, Benny has run through his entire family tree. He pulls the SUV to a stop in an empty parking lot and cocks his chin at me.

"I must have the wrong place," he says, sounding confused.

My heart swells to nearly bursting, and the words lodge in my throat. "No," I say. "This is it. The future home of Pancake Circus. How did you find it?"

Benny shifts in his seat and faces me. "It's important to you," he says quietly. "And even if I hated the idea at first, I want to be supportive. This is what you do. Why you're here."

He's quiet then, as if he's thinking what I'm thinking. It's why I'm only here for a short time.

"Looks pretty quiet. I expected contractors and construction and shit."

I nod. Yeah. Me too. Instead, I ask, "Want a tour?"

He kills the engine, and we cross the gravel lot. There used to be a restaurant here years ago. A place with a large parking lot and a drive-through, but it's long since been abandoned. Permits are taped to the dark front windows, but Benny is right. Other than that, there's no sign that a new business is well on its way to being born. It's a sad symbol of my life in a way—so much potential, so much hope. And now it's stuck, not quite what it was and nothing like what it could be.

I push all the conflicting thoughts away.

"Come on," I tell him. "Let's go inside."

He follows me to the front door, and I use the access code to unlock the lockbox, then I take the keys from it and unlock the front door.

Inside, the electricity is off, but we still have power running to the building, so I lead him back into the big kitchen and flip on all the lights.

Benny sucks in a deep breath. The place smells a little funky, like ammonia, mildew, and mice droppings. But the kitchen is huge, easily three times the size of Benito's. He runs his hand along the stainless-steel counters. They are in disrepair—banged-up from boxes and other items being put on the counters over the years when the place was not functional. Before Culinary

Capital bought it at auction, in part because of its distressed condition.

"You know," he says, "this place has been closed as long as I can remember."

"It was open until a few years ago as a private event space," I tell him, explaining what I know. "It used to be a…"

"A Papa Gino's Pizza." He snaps his fingers. "No freaking way. I remember now. Back when I was really little, I came to a few pizza parties here."

I nod. "The sisters who own the company I work for are the Ginetti sisters. When the franchise opened, their father envisioned a few locations that could have games and play areas like some of the big chains. This place started out as that." I smile. "Theresa still has one of the original arcade games in the office in Chicago. It doesn't work, but it's a symbol. A symbol of so many things. Dreams. Fun. Family."

Benny watches me as I talk, his eyes dark with something that I can't interpret. He is so, so pretty. His chin is lifted, that dimple winking at me as he listens. I've never felt bonded to a man this way before. It's as though he was made to be mine, and the invisible threads that connect us throb as I talk.

I know he wants to come closer to me. To touch me. To hold me tight while we share these memories, these very real parts of our lives. And yet, he just stands there, the electric tension between us sparking with lust and maybe so much more.

"So, then," I say, brightening my voice to try to shatter the stillness, "in its second life, Papa Gino's here was a drive-through hot dog and burger joint. That didn't last long, but the owners decided to hold on to it and keep it as private event space until about nine years ago. The place has been mostly abandoned since then."

Benny looks confused. "It's a wild coincidence that a Papa Gino's used to be here. Did the fact that their dad once owned this place factor into the decision to build here?"

I nod. "I think so. Maybe there was a little nostalgia behind the final decision, sure. Papa Gino, the real Papa Gino, was from Chicago, and he liked to bring his family to Michigan, Indiana, and Ohio for vacations. The owners of my company have been to Star Falls many times over the years. It's a special place, and when Pancake Circus came to us, we primarily looked for locations just like this in the Midwest."

"Locations like this," he says quietly, his voice simmering with heat. "Small towns with untapped potential?"

"Exactly," I say. I suck my lower lip into my mouth. Untapped potential. Like him, like me. Like us together. I don't say it, but it's like Benny feels it.

He finally crosses the kitchen and stands in front of me. He smooths a loose hair behind my ear, his fingers grazing my cheek. "Lucky me. You ended up here." The words hang heavy between us, like he wants to say more and is weighing exactly how to word it. But the raw emotion is clouded over, and his lips twist into a smirk. "Just think. You could be making out with some sandwich-maker in South Bend instead."

The laugh hits me hard. "Well, then I think I'm the

lucky one." I lace my arms around his waist and rest my head against his chest. Then I sigh and close my eyes.

He holds me close to him, rocking slightly to the hum of the electric lights overhead.

"So, why's it so quiet here?" he asks, his voice echoing in the silence.

I lift my chin and look up at him. "There have been some delays," I say cryptically.

My heart is pounding hard in my chest. I don't want to admit that everything is falling apart. That the project is about to get canceled. That I'm probably just days away from being pulled out of Star Falls.

"I'm sorry," he says. "I understand delays, all right." He rests his chin on the top of my head and holds me tighter. "Shit that doesn't get done but needs to—bills, repairs, and HR issues. Sometimes I feel like the longer I'm in business, the worse it gets. Things don't get easier over time, unless I'm just a major fucking moron who can't learn."

He pulls away from me and walks slowly through the kitchen, running his hands along the abandoned surfaces. I wonder if he, like me, can almost hear the ghosts of chefs who worked here, meals made and served. The smells and tastes of what this place could be are so real to me, I almost can't stand the silence.

Benny fills the space with his honesty. "I wish I'd known before I opened the restaurant what kind of shit I'd face." His brown eyes look sad, the dimple in his chin really pronounced as he frowns. "I just wanted to cook, you know? Make great meals. There's nothing better than the feeling of feeding people something they love.

But even more than that, I love food. I love the weight and texture of pasta dough in my hands. I love the precision of dicing a shallot for a glaze and seasoning something until it's just right."

He laughs, sounding bitter but not angry. More like, resigned.

"I'm so good at what I love, and everything else…" He groans and then leans his butt back against the counter and runs a hand through his hair. He's wearing a lightweight forest-green puffer coat, and the sleeves make a swishing sound as he moves his arm. "Can I be brutally fucking honest?" he asks. "Real talk?"

"Yes," I whisper. I want him to be. I'm hoping he'll say something that will make it easier for me to open up to him. Because I have to, and the sooner I do, the better.

"Willow." When he says my name, he sounds pained. "I suck at running my business. My books are a mess. The only thing that stops me from getting the utilities shut off is the friends I have who work for the city. They know I'll pay when they remind me. I always do. But I just can't even get ahead of the thousand things there are to do."

He tugs on the ends of his hair and paces long strides through the empty kitchen. "I want to be as good as I am at food with everything, but I'm not. I can't be. I fucking suck at everything that is not food." His voice rises, and he sounds like he's unburdening himself as he vents. He points at me. "That community development grant? The one Mags is pissed at me about? I desperately need the money. No lie. I don't have the cash for a new roof. And if that roof makes it through the winter, it'll be a fucking miracle. If it doesn't, then what? Health inspector shuts me down?"

As I watch him pace in increasingly frantic circles through the massive kitchen, my heart catches in my chest. I have heard this same complaint time after time, year after year. People who love the passion of the work but not the drudgery of it. I get it. I understand it. All that other stuff is actually stuff I'm great at. My entire career has been filled with chefs like Benny.

What my entire career hasn't been filled with is men like him. Men who make my heart tighten in my chest with a look. Men who would bring me home to their parents, walk in on those parents having sex, and stick around for coffee and conversation. Men who make kale ravioli so delicious, I knew from the first bite I would never taste anything like it and I would never tire of it.

Benny leans back against the counter, dropping his shoulders in defeat. "I'm in so deep, Willow. Not debt, thank God. I don't overspend, but I'm right there, right on the edge. I make enough to cover my people, my rent, and my costs. But extras? What restaurant owner has the time to take off to spend with their families, friends? I don't have that kind of flexibility, let alone the money to go on vacation, take a real break. But I'm missing out. Life is passing me by. I know I'm only thirty-one, but when I thought for real my pops could be sick…" He rubs his eyes hard, like he's holding back tears. "I haven't spent enough time with him. I don't want to lose my family even though I'm right fucking here. And I don't want to lose my restaurant."

I join him, wrapping my arms around his waist and leaning my face against his warm chest. The heat of him radiates through his flannel shirt and puffer coat, and I breathe it in. He's talented—more so than me, I'm sure of that. I was never a great cook. I just loved doing it. That's why I found my place around food and not in a kitchen of my own.

None of this should ever work, but a small part of me sparks with an idea. But first, I need to tell him the truth.

"I went to Cleveland yesterday to meet with a roofing contractor," I say, my voice low, my cheek pressed to his chest. "I wanted to see if I could use any of my connections to negotiate a lower price on a roof for you."

Benny puts his hands on my shoulders and moves me away from him, not in a rough way, but so he can look into my eyes. "You did what? Why? Why would you do that?"

I give him a small smile. "Because I knew you weren't going to apply for the grant, and I know you need the roof." I shrug. "I didn't get very far. I was able to get one of the contractors working here to pull the last permit on the roof you have now." I sigh, because what I have to tell him, I'm sure he already knows. "Your landlord kind of screwed you. The roof that you're supposed to replace should have been replaced eight years ago. When you signed your lease, he probably knew you'd need to replace the roof before the lease was up."

Benny's mouth drops open. "I had a lawyer look it over," he says. "I even had an inspection…"

I nod. "I'm sure it's all aboveboard. There's a lot of wiggle room in this stuff. A couple of warm winters and maybe that roof would last five years longer than expected. But with the last couple of years you've had here in Ohio…"

I press my hips to his and cup his face in my hands. "The contractor I met with yesterday is booked solid through July. He said with how bad the last few winters have been, he can give you a discount and get you on the schedule, but if anything happens this winter, you'll be looking at a patchwork job. Maybe closing the restaurant until it's up to code. Hard to say, but with how wet the fall has been, he didn't want to commit to getting a job that big done as a rush. And definitely not cheap."

I lean forward and place a light kiss on his lips. "I'm sorry. I tried."

Benny's eyes darken, and he lowers his brows. "You did that for me?"

I nod. "Well, I didn't do much but look into the options. I didn't solve anything."

Benny then takes my face in his hands and strokes my lower lip with his thumb. "You went out of your way to help me. You got your contacts involved. You put yourself out there for me."

I lower my chin so I can kiss his thumb lightly. "It's what all of us who care about you would do," I tell him. "Mags, me, Jasmine, Sassy, Rita, your parents. You're surrounded by a lot of love, Benny. Sometimes it might just be hard to see it for what it is."

He smirks that sexy, confident smile that sends my heart into my stomach, and heat floods through my body. "You think Mags and Rita love me? I mean, I know I'm the sexiest single man in Star Falls, but…" He strokes my cheek. "I have the only woman I want."

I look up into his face. "I don't know what to say, Benny," I whisper. "I love spending time with you, but I'm a short-timer. I'm leaving soon. And I'm more than ten years older than you. You really think this could work out? I mean, like, long-term? What about kids? You mean you don't want to give your parents more little Bianchis to look after?"

I feel tears burning the backs of my eyes now. I don't regret any of my decisions. I never wanted kids. Not after the childhood I had. And I never believed I could want a man who wanted anything different from what I wanted.

But now, I don't know.

Maybe I could want the man. I just don't know where that leaves the things that he might want.

"Willow, family is about so much more than kids." He holds my face so our eyes meet. "Don't get me wrong. If the right woman came along and she wanted a ton of babies, that'd be a decision that we'd make together. Time, money, all that shit would go into it. But if the right woman came along and kids were not on the table, you think I'd throw away the woman I love for something I don't even know if I want?"

I back away. Whoa. Love. Love… He said it, and it's far too soon for that.

"Slow down," he says, stepping close to me. "You look like I probably did when I saw my dad's dick."

I am trying to relax. Trying to let my brain work this out.

He leans down and kisses me on the lips, a light, sweet kiss. "Baby, I've known you were special since the moment I met you. I am falling in love with you."

"Benny, it's been…"

"I know," he says. "But tell me something. How did you feel when you ate my ravioli?"

I curve my lips into a frown. "That's not the same as—"

"Willow," he presses. "Say it. What did you feel?"

"I loved it," I admit. "It was unlike anything I've ever had. I knew from the moment I tasted it, I could eat it a thousand times and never get sick of it."

He nods. "I'm a simple man. I know what I like. I know what I feel. I'm not asking you for forever, but I'm asking you to consider dating me. Fuck the one-year rule or whatever. Who knows how you'll feel by the time this project is over." He waves a hand around the kitchen and smirks. "Shit, at this rate, you'll be in Star Falls for the next three years. Who knows? A couple more construction delays, and you might end up staying a lifetime."

His grin is so warm, so genuine, tears fill my eyes. "I'm not that simple," I tell him. "Nothing about me is that easy. My past, my present."

He nods. "I know we're different. I know that you're

classy and I'm all ego. I'm not good with numbers, and look at you." He motions his hands around the kitchen again. "You do this. This is your job."

He's not wrong. We're so different, and yet, every comfortable moment of the last two months I've spent with him.

Every night, I've fallen asleep in his arms. Every morning, I've woken up beside him. We've talked about surface things, but he's a man I can go to with anything. I know that I can, and worse, I know that I want to. Deep down, maybe everything I tell myself about why this can't work are just bullshit excuses. A way for me to run from something more real than anything else I've known.

"What are you saying?" I ask, because I don't know what else to say. That I love him? That I'm falling in love with him? Hell yeah, I probably am.

But the timing couldn't be worse. This could never work. Just like Pancake Circus, one major snag and the whole thing would fall apart in my hands.

"Willow, all I'm saying is that I'm falling for you. I think about you constantly. I used to spend every waking minute thinking about my restaurant and food, and now I spend every waking minute thinking about my restaurant and food and you. I want it all. I want you as part of my life, and I want to think about a future that lasts longer than a project. Will you at least consider it? I'm not asking you to marry me. Hell, I'm not even asking you to stay here in Star Falls or to give up your job."

He pulls me close and crushes me against his chest.

"I never want you to choose between something you love and someone you love. Just tell me you're in this with me. Whatever that means. Is that asking too much?"

That's the question.

I can't face the reality that this project is going to fail and I'm going to be on a plane in a few days or a few weeks, and then I'll be the one to have to make the choice.

I know he says he's not asking me to make a choice, but he's not going to give up his business, and I wouldn't ask him to.

But I'm not ready to give up everything that I've worked my entire life for because of love.

His hold on me loosens, and he looks guarded. He searches my face for his answer. "Willow? Whatever this means, are you in this with me? Not just hooking up, no fuck buddies. I want to know you're mine for as long as you'll have me. If that means after this project is over, you leave the state, we'll find a way if we still want that. I'm not asking for then. I'm asking you for right now. Are we doing this, you and I?"

Tears wet my eyelashes. "Do you mean dinners with your family? Dates? The whole nine?"

He nods. "Everything except surprise visits with my parents. I might have to start calling first."

I laugh and step into his arms. I rest my face against his chest and listen to the beating of his heart. It's fast and steady, like mine. I close my eyes and let my fears roar through my ears.

This will never work! the fears shout.

Though this time, with Benny's arms around me, a tiny voice inside me asks back, *But what if it does?*

But I'm leaving. My rational brain insists on seeing the facts.

You have long-distance relationships with everyone you love, my heart reminds me.

But I'm so, so scared, my head finally admits.

I look up at Benny and reveal the truth. "I'm scared. Scared this could work. Scared how much I want you. Scared that it's all too much, too soon. Scared it can't last."

"Be scared with me, then, Willow. Not of me. Not of this. I'll never hold you back, but I don't want to let you go."

I close my eyes and lift up on my toes. Every ounce of my heart, body, and strength is pulling me—not away from him, but toward. Is this too much? Too soon? Probably all of it. But maybe for the first time in my life, I've met someone who's worth trying for.

"Okay," I whisper. "I'd rather be afraid with you than let you go. I'm in it, Benny. I'm in this—whatever it is, for however long it lasts."

CHAPTER 17
BENITO

"WE HAVE twenty minutes before I have to leave for the restaurant." As soon as I close the door to my condo behind us, I have Willow pressed against the door.

"Plenty of time," she breathes, already tugging at the bottom of her sweatshirt.

I unzip my jeans and kick off my shoes, then throw myself against her, pressing my chest against hers. Her top is off, only a paper-thin bra separating us.

"Mine," I growl, shoving aside the fabric of her cup and sucking her nipple deep into my mouth. "This is mine, and this…" With my mouth occupied on her breast, I bend down and grab her ass with both hands. "Willow, you're fucking perfect. Your body, your…"

"Less talking, more sucking," she begs, arching her back.

I swirl the tip of my tongue over her hard nipple, scraping the peak with my top teeth in my frenzy to taste her, claim her. I've fucked her almost every day since I met her, but every time I kiss her, it's like a hunger inside me demanding more, more, more. I'll never get sick of this. I'll never get enough of her.

She whimpers my name as I graze my teeth lightly across her flesh. "Benny…"

I move my mouth from her tits to her lips, and she grabs my head, fisting my hair with greedy hands. We feast on each other's mouths, tasting and prodding, our tongues clashing like two people who've been starved for each other.

This is just part of why I know I'm falling in love with Willow Watkins. I can't imagine being with a woman who doesn't ignite my body and stimulate my brain. She's everything. Not just a snack. She's sustenance. And I want to devour her, consume her.

My cock is throbbing inside my briefs, and I pant kisses into Willow's mouth while she strokes me through the soft fabric. "My bed," I groan. "Now."

She starts to move, but I stop her by sweeping her into my arms.

"Benny." She laughs, but she wraps her arms around my neck and buries her face against my cheek. We try to kiss as I stumble toward my room with her in my arms, but I can't see, and I smack her knee into the door frame.

"Oh my God." My eyes fly open at the sound. "I'm so sorry. Are you okay?"

She's laughing and waves me forward. "I'm fine, keep going. I'm fine."

Both of us laughing, I set her gently down on the bed, and she lies back, watching as I shed the last of my clothes.

"You have like fifteen minutes," she says, her eyes wide. There is a flush across her chest that I want to lick, shoulder to shoulder, neck to navel. For a minute, I seriously consider calling in to work. I've never done it. Never blown off work for anyone. And I can't start now. That would be a very dangerous habit. Knowing how I feel about Willow, Benito's would be closed by Christmas.

"More than enough time," I say.

I run my hands up her thighs, grip the waistband of her yoga pants, and tug them and her panties off in one pull. One of her breasts is poking out from her bra cup, and her pussy is bare for me, her legs open and waiting.

She's the most delicious sight I've ever seen.

I drop onto the bed and lie on top of her, positioning my throbbing cock between her legs. "I want you in every way possible. I want this forever," I grunt, nudging my cock against her drenched entrance. "Tell me you want this, Willow. I want to hear you say you want me."

"Fuck yes, I want you," she says, her hands clawing at my ass. "Fuck me, Benny. God, I need this. I need you."

That's all I need to hear. I piston my hips and drive all the way inside her so fast and so deep, we both cry out. The pleasure is so exquisite, so complete, I have to slow myself down or I'll pound her until I come. And I want more than that for her.

"Fuck me," I tell her. "Move, baby."

She's underneath me, but she widens her legs and I hold her knees open with my palms. She thrusts her hips up while I roll mine in time with hers, our movements so frantic, so rushed, my balls slap against her ass. She wriggles and moans, gasps and begs me for more, harder, and I give her everything I have.

Everything I know she wants.

In and out, in and out, I press her knees wider, opening her more, my cock driving deep until finally she screams my name. "Benny. Oh fuck."

I feel the walls of her pussy tighten around me, milking my cock. She's so wet, I have to grit my teeth and curl my toes to hold back just a little longer. She's crying, tears on her cheeks, moaning my name as she jerks her hips harder against mine. "So good," she murmurs. "You feel so fucking good."

Her breathing is ragged, her beautiful lips dry from panting, and a sheen of sweat breaks out across her hairline. I lean down and claim her mouth, kissing her and releasing her knees. I support my weight with my arms, but as soon as she claws at my back, pulling me closer, rubbing her tits against my chest, I lose it, lose every ounce of control. I fall off the cliff, coming hard and hot deep inside her.

"Fuck," I roar, banging into her so hard the bed rocks back and forth on the hardwood floor.

I ride my orgasm, the climax so powerful my toes cramp and my hair is drenched with sweat. The come-down is slow, and before I know it, I feel Willow's nails scratching through my hair.

"Babe." I can hear her whisper to me, but fuck, I'm wrecked.

"Mm-hm," I grumble, my face smashed between her tits. This is heaven. I'm sure of it. I'm dead, and this is the eternal happiness I've somehow earned. I'm never, ever moving.

"Benny, you have to get to the restaurant, babe." She scratches my scalp in long, relaxing strokes. If she thinks that's going to get my heavy-ass legs moving, she's so wrong.

"Five minutes," I mumble, drooling on her, but my cock is still inside her. I'm warm with her underneath me. God, this feels like bliss. All I could ever want. More than I've ever had before.

As I'm lying there, her nails bringing my head a new level of happy, I can't stop the words. They echo in my thoughts, coming from a place deep in my chest.

I love this. I love you.

I love you.

The thought has my eyes flying open. Did I say it out loud?

I look up at her, her flushed face pink and smiling. "Hey there, gorgeous."

She doesn't look spooked, so I take a long, slow breath.

"You are amazing," she says, tapping a finger on the tip of my nose. "And you're going to be late."

"Worth it," I say, reluctantly pulling my semihard cock from inside her and rolling over. "Fuck, I hate leaving you."

"I hate that you have to go," she says, a satisfied smile on her face.

"Stay here as long as you want," I tell her. "In fact, please promise me you'll be here when I get home."

She grins. "I have to go home and shower. I have work emails I have to…"

I hold up a hand. "I'm going to leave a spare key on the counter. Just promise me you'll be back here in my bed waiting for me when I get home from work."

I lean down to kiss her smiling face. She is perfect. Sweet, sexy, smart. Mine. "I'll be here," she promises.

Then I take the world's fastest shower and run off to what is now the second love of my life—my business.

I arrive in record time to find the place unusually busy. Rita offers me a quick wave as she seats a handful of late lunch diners, and when I check in with Jas at the bar, she gives me a weird look.

"You look happy," she says. "What's the big smile about?"

There is warmth in her words, and I smile even bigger.

"Nothing," I tell her, although that's a fucking lie.

I'm in love.

I'm happy.

The world has never seemed brighter. Now, if I could just block out all the shit that causes me stress.

Well, that ain't happening, as I can already tell from the look on Jas's face. She leans forward on the bar and motions me to come close with a hand.

"Well, you might want to hold on to that smile," she says. "Mags is waiting for you in your office."

The warmth and satisfaction of my morning with

Willow fade away like someone splashed me in the face with a bucket of stinky mop water.

"Thanks, Jas." I nod, then head into the kitchen to check on the staff.

Carla and Duncan are managing the lunch orders just fine. The controlled chaos calms me, and it's hard not to think back to the kitchen at the old Papa Gino's place. What I wouldn't do to expand my business. Make it bigger, better. I love this crusty old location, but after six years here, the lure of something new does have some appeal.

But I watch my kitchen run like a tiny but tight machine, and I say a little prayer of thanks for what I do have. I have so much. Someday I'll get my shit together and can maybe dream about more. But until I've earned it, this is Benito's. This is me.

I make my way down the back hallway toward my office, where I find the door open, Mags sitting in the same chair in front of my desk where she was before. She jumps to her feet when I walk in.

"Mags," I say, not able to stop the scowl from covering my face. "I thought you wanted some time off."

She nods, and her face looks pale, her eyes puffy. "I did. But I didn't want to leave things where they were yesterday. Benny, I don't want you to fire me. And I don't want to leave."

I throw my hands in the air. "Mags, I'm not the one who started all this shit. You're the one who's unhappy. What do you want from me? You want a job? You got it. But I'm not going back to—"

She holds up a hand. "I'm sorry to interrupt. I know.

I've been out of line. It's not anything you've done or anything you've done differently. It's just…" She looks at me through her lashes, lowering her head. "A couple weeks ago, a city guy came out to read the gas meter and made a really shitty comment about you. About you not paying your bills."

A flood of anger flows through my limbs. "Who was it?" I ask. "Did you talk to the guy? Get his name?"

She shakes her head. "He was new. I've never seen him before, and I was so stunned, I didn't know what to say."

I think about this for a second. "Where did this happen? Where were you when he said this?"

Mags looks down at her hands. "He was at the bar. After he read the meter, he ordered lunch to go. I threw some extra focaccia in for him and thought I'd do something nice, you know, his being a city worker and all. I brought it out to him, and as I was handing it over, he made that shitty comment."

My blood is boiling. "Who else heard him? He said this in front of customers?"

Mags's face goes pale. "Yeah. Lunch rush. Jas heard, and Sassy for sure. I don't know how many diners, but it was pretty awkward."

I slam my ass into my seat, wondering how long I'd get locked up for beating the shit out of a city worker. There's probably an extra penalty for crimes like that, but maybe in my defense, I could claim he was damaging my business's reputation.

"Fuck," I sigh, the anger suddenly draining out of me.

As I think back on the last few weeks, I start piecing it all together. I let the delivery guys go and have been doing a lot more work myself. Sassy and Jas whispering on their breaks. A new restaurant coming to town, even if it's not open yet. Mags probably saw the writing on the wall. Benito's is in trouble, even I refused to see the signs.

"So, that is what all this has been about?" I ask. "You're afraid I'm about to go under?"

Mags shrugs. "I didn't know, not for sure. But you're so goddamn stubborn, Benny. You don't let anyone in. I've been here with you for years now, years of my life. Day in, day out. You call me your right hand, yet I don't know anything about the business. Nothing real. If we were in trouble, I'd probably be the last one to know." She meets my eyes, a challenge in her look. "If something was going on here, something serious, would you tell me first? Or would I be the last to know because you'd need me more than everybody else?"

I rub my eyes, and it hits me. She's right. I've been an arrogant, selfish bastard to the people who most deserve my trust. And it's all because I'm scared. Scared they will leave me once they know the truth. That one crack in the facade and the whole goddamn place will fall down around my feet.

"You're right about so many things, Mags," I tell her. "I need help. Benito's is not in trouble. I'm in trouble. I'm overwhelmed. I'm shit at paperwork and staying organized and creating a budget." I shake my head. "I don't want to ask for help because I don't want to admit that I'm a failure. This place is my life. It's all I ever wanted. What kind of man am I if I can't run this place myself?"

Mags laughs. "You're a typical man," she scoffs. Then she leans forward in her chair. "Benny, it's not a sin to ask for help. Look at you and all the people you help. Rita, for one." She presses her lips together and looks pained. "I shouldn't have said what I did about Rita yesterday. I've been feeling like an asshole about it. She's a great lady, and the customers love her. But you're the person who gave a very old lady the only job in town she could get. Why? Because she's good for the business? No. Because you can help her. That's the kind of man you are, Benny. Yes, you're arrogant and cocky and all the rest, but you're also a truly good, good person. I wouldn't want to work for anyone else."

She leans back in her chair. "I'm sorry I haven't dealt with any of this well. But I'd like to stay. I'd like to take on more responsibility. I'll do the books, or I'll just set up your bills on autopay. Whatever you want. I don't need to make more money, not at first. Can you try giving me more responsibility, and if it works out, can we talk about a bigger role for me here?"

I sigh. "I'm not going to make it easy on you," I admit. "I'm stubborn, and I hate being told what to do."

"Don't I fucking know it," she chuckles. "And yet, I'm here. And it's technically my day off."

I think about Willow. About the fact that she's only here for a year. How I have a ticking clock and want to spend every minute of the time we have together. Making whatever we have work so that she is sure what we have is real. Because even now, with Mags in my office, a restaurant full of customers, and a kitchen I really need to get into, my thoughts are of Willow. My body misses her. Wants her. Can't wait to get home to her.

And then, of course, there's my family. More help with my work means more time with them too. It's a win-win. That just means that I actually have to do it. Open up to someone. Admit the things I suck at. I have to be okay with failing. Because if I let Mags take over or even just pitch in with parts of my business, I have to accept that it's because I can't do it all.

I know it's true.

It's about time I get honest about it.

"All right," I tell her. "You want a title and a pay raise; you'll need to show me we have the money for that. And I'm going to let you write up the job description, figure out the schedule, all that shit. There's a lot I'm terrible at, Mags. And you're going to see the real mess I've made. That scare you?"

She beams like I just promised her a partnership. "No. I was scared not knowing what was going on. I'm up for the challenge of cleaning shit up."

I hold up my hand in warning. "But look, you're going to get mad. You're going to get frustrated. You're going to think, this is so fucking easy, why doesn't he just do this or that. And that's going to shut me down and piss me off."

She nods solemnly. "But you know I can't lie to you, Benito. I have to call you out on your stupid shit."

I arch a brow at her. "This ain't going to be easy. I'm just warning you. My ego's on the line here."

"I know." She's quiet then. "It would be a blow for anyone's ego to have to own up to stuff they can't handle and ask for help. I'll do my best not to make it too personal. And I won't take it personally if things get heated."

I slap my hands on the desk and stand from my chair. I hold out a hand to her. "If I didn't trust you, Mags, this wouldn't be happening. Thanks for having my back even when I didn't see it or acknowledge it."

She shakes my hand and turns to leave. "Oh," she says. "Since I'm here, you want me to stay?"

I'm tempted. If she stays, I can go home to Willow. Home to tell her everything that I'm going to fix. Everything that I'm determined to make work. But then I look at Mags. Every choice I make from here on out, I'm going to try to do the right thing. Not going with what's easy or what pleases me.

As much as I want to let her close so I can spend time with Willow, I need to give Mags some time off. I need to make a little progress in my office so I'm ready for her help tomorrow. I know what I need to do, and for once, I'm going to say yes to the shit I hate doing. I'm going to face it and do it.

"No," I tell her, shaking my head. "You get out of here. Take the day off. You want to work tomorrow, I'll see you when we're both fresh."

She nods and gives me a smile as she leaves. Then, since Carla and Duncan are covering the kitchen, I open my desk drawer and pull out the laptop that I use so rarely, it's not even charged, and I get to work.

CHAPTER 18
WILLOW

AFTER BENNY LEAVES FOR WORK, I make his bed and grab the spare key from the kitchen counter. I lock his unit behind me and head home, braced for what's coming.

I check my email and see I have close to fifty new messages and an invitation to a meeting with Theresa for tomorrow morning. I send Alex an instant message and ask if Theresa is free now.

Alex: Let me check with her assistant. One sec.

While I wait for Alex to reply, I wander over to the huge glass windows that overlook the river. I stare out into space until the pinging of the IM system brings me back to the moment.

Alex: She wants to talk now. Just to you. Can you jump on?

I confirm that I can, quickly smoothing my hair back into a bun and peeking at my reflection in the camera on my phone. I look fine. From the neck up, there will be no signs that I just got fucked within an inch of my life by the most amazing man. The most amazing chef. The reason I might consider something very different for my life.

I click on the meeting invite that Alex sent, and within seconds, Theresa's furious face fills the screen.

"It's fucking done," she says quietly. "Pardon my language, but all this work, all the time they spent pursuing us. I'm pissed off. So much waste. The Kincades filed an injunction to stop work on the property in Star Falls," she tells me without preamble. Without so much as even a hello. "It's over, Willow. Pancake Circus is dead. I'll announce the news to the team in the meeting tomorrow, but since you reached out, I figured I'd give you a heads-up."

I knew this outcome was inevitable, but hearing it from Theresa's mouth sours my stomach. "Thank you," I say. "And I'm sorry."

I have nothing to be sorry about, of course. None of this has anything to do with me, and yet the only word to describe how I feel is sorry. Sorry that my company will lose valuable time and an enormous amount of money while we fight this out with the Kincades in the legal system. Sorry that this means my time in Star Falls is officially coming to an end.

"No point in having Alex make your travel plans back to Chicago," Theresa says, her voice frustrated. "I don't have another site set up for you yet, so you might as well stay in Star Falls while we have the lease on that condo you're staying in. Unless you have someplace else you'd like to stay. I'd love to have you back in the office to strategize and meet with our attorneys. Are you all right staying there until we figure out our next steps?"

I nod. "Of course. But I'd like to take a little time off, if you're okay with it."

Theresa nods. "How much time are you thinking?" she asks.

I calculate the distance in my head, the idea starting to take shape. "Two weeks, tops." I rush on to explain, so she doesn't jump to any incorrect conclusions. "One of my best friends is on bed rest, about to have her first baby as a single mom. I'd like to visit her while things are settling down."

She nods. "All right. Make sure Alex knows your schedule. You may have to take calls with our attorneys while you're away, but I'll do what I can to accommodate your time off."

"Theresa," I say, before she's able to end the meeting. It's just me and her, my boss. The woman I've worked for and whose company has given me purpose for…well, maybe for too long. "Thank you," I tell her. "I love what I do. I believe in what we do as a company. And I am just sorry that things have turned out this way."

Theresa nods, but I can tell she's stressed, angry, and probably scared. This deal going south is going to cost the company millions. There's just no putting a positive spin on that. "Enjoy your time off, Willow."

Then, without a goodbye, she ends the meeting. I immediately pick up the phone and call Jessa. She answers on the first ring.

"Do you have a radar for tears or something now?" she asks, sounding weepy and miserable. "Or maybe I just cry all the time and only notice it when you call?"

We're not on video, but my heart clenches at her sniffles. "Jessa," I say gently. "Would now be a good time to come visit you? I can stay in a hotel if I'll be in the way."

"Oh my God," she wails, literally wails into the phone. "How soon can you get here?"

I grin, and tears wet my lashes. "Okay, calm down. I haven't booked anything, and I can't stay long. I need to take a trip for work, but I'm thinking by the end of the week. Possibly sooner."

We hash out the details, and I even talk to Jessa's mom, who sounds grateful to have someone coming by to help. After I end the call, I send an email to Theresa confirming I'll attend the meeting with the team in the morning, but that I'll be out of the office for one to two weeks after. I add a line at the end of my email with a request.

Theresa, I know we're going to have to communicate to the contractors that the work will stop. Is it possible you'd let me handle that personally? I've been working with these companies and would like to preserve the relationships if I can. You never know what might happen. If we settle, etc., we'll want to keep the same team in place. And I'd like to be the one to soften the blow if I can.

She replies back with one sentence. *As long as the lawyers say it's okay, yes.*

That's good enough for me. I start to get excited, quickly checking airfare and booking a flight out of Cleveland tomorrow night. I'm not sure that I can fix any of this. But I have a plan to try.

I spend the rest of the afternoon packing my bags

and cleaning my place. On my counter is the white flower dish that came with the bouquet Benny gave me the day after we met. What a long time ago that seems like now, but really, it's only been a matter of months. But during that time, I've changed. I've opened up to things that I never thought I wanted. I only hope that this is what I truly want. This is a lot to think about…too much, really.

But for the first time in my life, I'm curious what might happen, what new adventures and exciting firsts I can experience if I ditch the one-year plan. If I stop chasing new dreams. If I set down roots and let myself finally find a place I can call home.

Now I just have to break it to Benny that I'm leaving.

I spend the afternoon running around Star Falls. I make a stop at the very small mall to pick up the sexiest lingerie I can find. I buy a bottle of champagne and two flutes, then stop at the florist to buy two red roses. I want tonight to be special. It will be our last night together for a while, and I don't know what will happen when I talk to Benny about my plans. Will he still want to date, knowing that I'm leaving? Knowing that my plan might not work?

I want to be prepared to make it special. Especially if this is really, truly the end for us. I don't want to think that it could be, not after everything he said. But something like this could be too much for a new relationship to manage. I have to brace myself for whatever happens.

When Benny arrives home, it's well after ten. As promised, I'm in his bed. There is a bottle of champagne chilling by the bedside, along with the flutes. I plucked the red petals from the roses and sprinkled them in a path from the front door to the bedroom, which was dark except for the warm, flickering orange glow of a bunch of candles.

I'm lying on top of the bed, my entire body covered head to toe in comfy pajamas and socks. Underneath, I'm wearing the very naughty items I bought at the mall, but I want to leave that little tidbit as a surprise.

"Babe?" I hear him call as he locks the front door.

He follows the rose petals to the bed and leans down to kiss me. "What's all this?" He takes in the candles and the roses, a grin on his gorgeous face.

My heart seizes in my chest. He looks tired but happy. A lock of hair flops over his forehead, and I reach up and push it back.

"I smell like I just took a swim in garlic sauce," he says, sniffing. "Give me two minutes to shower."

I pop the cork on the champagne and fill two glasses, then when I hear the water turn on, I slide under the covers and take off the warm socks that cover the thigh-high red stockings I'm wearing under my pajama pants. I lean back and listen to the water running through the pipes. I think about what I'm going to tell Benny. Where to start. It's not going to be easy, but if he is half the man I believe he is, things will be okay.

He comes out of the bathroom a few minutes later,

his hair damp and a loose pair of pajama pants riding low on his waist. He is stunning. Beautiful. His face lights up with a cocky smile, and he takes a running start and then dives into the bed on top of me.

He lands with a crash, shifting the bed on the floor, and we both burst out laughing. He nods at the champagne. "You've been busy today," he says, kissing me once, twice, then three times on the lips. "Mm, fucking delicious. So, what are we celebrating?"

I lean over and grab a flute, then hand him one and take the other. I hold mine up and offer a toast. "Well, to both of us failing and then rising like phoenixes."

He looks confused. "I don't get it, but I'll drink to it."

We clink glasses, take a sip, and then I set both flutes on the bedside table beside us.

"So," I say, leaning back against the pillows. "Pancake Circus is dead. But I have a plan to bring it back to life."

"What?" He widens his eyes, and his mouth drops open. "Willow, what does that mean? What happened?"

I explain about the Kincade family backing out for reasons that they haven't shared. How the injunction will possibly stop construction and tie up any progress on the project until the long legal battle is sorted out.

"But," I say, "I've lived and breathed this project for two years. I know this will work. We just have to get the place open." That's when I look at him. "I booked a flight down to Florida. I leave tomorrow. I'm going to the original location, and I'm going to stay there until the owners agree to talk to me."

"Can you do that?" he asks. "What about the lawyers?"

"Technically, my company can't communicate with the family except through their lawyers, but I'm not personally named in anything that I've seen yet. As far as I know, it's a loophole. I need to know, Benny. I need to know why they want out and what I can do to make this happen."

Benny lowers his brows and reaches past me for another sip of champagne. "What if you can't change their minds?" he asks. "Holy fuck, Willow. I'm just getting it now. You'll leave, won't you? You'll have no reason to stay in Star Falls."

"I do have many reasons to stay in Star Falls," I say. "I just need to work out why this is happening. I need to understand so I can make a good decision about what I want to do next."

His face darkens, and he rolls onto his side to face me. "What does that mean?" he asks. "What you want to do next. That means where you'll go next. What city, what project. You're leaving me."

He looks so sad, so broken. And my own heart cracks open just a bit at the realization. It's one thing to know that I might leave. It's another to face that it's happening right now.

"I have some ideas," I say. "But I can't make any decisions until I have the work stuff sorted out." I reach for his face, smooth his damp hair back. "Benny, I've never been a relationship person. I'm a short-timer. One year here, another there." I meet his dark eyes. "But you've made me rethink what kind of person I really am. What kind of person I could be."

I pull my hand away from him, a sudden flush of vulnerability making me feel very, very exposed.

"I'm afraid to admit how much I think I want this," I whisper. "You make me want to experience new adventures. The kind I can have by staying in one place. By staying with one person. But I'm scared."

He scoots closer to me and rests his head on my thigh. I lean back against the pillow and stroke his hair, and we're quiet for a minute. The candles flicker and burn, filling the room with the light fragrances of vanilla and something heavier, like sandalwood.

"I did something terrifying today," he says. "I told Mags she could help me with more work at the restaurant. I need help, and I fucking admitted it."

His damp hair feels soft between my fingers, and I lightly scratch his scalp as I touch him. "And?" I ask. "Was that the right decision? How do you feel now?"

He absently runs a hand along my thigh and closes his eyes under my soft touch. He sighs. "I still feel terrified. But something's got to give, and I'll never know if I don't try."

He stops suddenly, his fingers tracing along the leg of my pajamas. "Wait a second," he says. "What's this?"

I grin. He's felt the seam of the thigh-highs I'm wearing under my pajamas. "This is my attempt at admitting the truth, no matter how scary it is."

We rearrange ourselves on the bed. Benny sits with his back against the pillows, and I straddle his lap. His eyes immediately go to the bright red fabric on my toes. Before I even touch him, before I even take off a single stitch of clothing, I see his dick start to tent the front of his pajamas.

"We're very different, Benny," I tell him, slowly unbuttoning the front of my pajama shirt. "In some ways. But in other ways, we're so very much alike."

I watch his face as he stares at my fingers as the first button opens.

"I've never been in love. Not really. Never had a family. I have, of course, but not really. I've never had a home—not a permanent one. But being with you makes me want all those things. It's terrifying. It's stressful. It's confusing." I unbutton the rest of the buttons and let the soft gray pajama top fall open. "But I can't think of anyone else I'd want to do all of that with."

"What else do you want to do with me?" he asks, his voice thick and raw. His eyes follow my movements as I wiggle out of my top. And then, he asks, "What is all this?"

"A little goodbye present," I say. "I'm going to be gone at least a week, and I wanted to make sure you had something to remember me by."

"Take off those pants," he growls. "I want to burn the image of all of you in all of that onto my brain forever."

I climb off the bed and let the pajama pants fall to the floor, then I turn around and give him a view of the outfit I bought today. A sheer black bustier encases my breasts in lace, delicate red roses embroidered over my nipples. A matching thong and garters barely cover my lower half, and since the tiny Star Falls mall was sold out of black thigh-high hose, I'm wearing bright-red fishnets.

"It's the best I could do on short notice," I tell him, spinning in a circle to show off the backside and the front.

"For fuck's sake, Willow." Benny practically lunges out of bed and pounces on me. His mouth, hot and breathless, immediately clamps down on my hip. "I want to taste every inch of you in this getup."

His fingers trail over the teeny-tiny fabric of the thong. Then his hands are everywhere, stroking my thighs, touching the fishnets, kissing and nibbling, grazing and licking until my knees go weak and I have to lie down on the bed.

"Ass to me," he demands.

He doesn't have to ask twice. I lift my ass in the air, and he reaches around my waist to tug the thong off. "We don't need this. Everything else is fucking perfect."

Somehow, after a lot of maneuvering and laughter, he gets the thong past the garters, and I'm bare to him, kneeling with my ass in the air while he licks my pussy from behind. He licks me in long, slow strokes, sucking my lips lightly into his mouth. My arms go weak, and my eyes flutter shut as I give in to the pleasure, the all-consuming bliss that is his mouth on my most sensitive parts.

But I don't want this to end too soon, so I turn around and motion for him to lose the pajama pants. He does and then sits back on the bed, his back to the pillows. I kneel with my legs wide open over his ankles and slowly inch my way up his body. I sit in his lap, carefully positioning his massive hard-on between us but far away from my needy pussy. I want to ride him, want him deep inside me. But not yet.

With my ass high in the air so he can see it, I dip my head low and take his cock into my mouth. I hum against his heat, working my hand around his shaft in time with my deep, slow sucking.

He whimpers, grunts, his hands fisting my hair and urging me up and back, up and down. I love the feel of him. The scratch of his soft hairs against my skin as I offer him all the pleasure I can bring.

I'm flooded with need, clenching with every pass. I want to share this pleasure with him. Give it and take my own. I lift my face and am about to climb onto his lap when he holds my face in his hands.

"I fucking love you, Willow Watkins," he grits out. "I love you."

I don't say anything. I don't feel like I have to. He knows how I feel. He knew how I felt long before I knew. And I do know. I know that whatever happens in the future, I've never wanted anyone more. I've never wanted a man's body, his business, his companionship, and his comfort more than I want all that with Benito Bianchi.

I climb on top of him, letting him enter me inch by agonizingly slow inch. He slams his head back against the headboard, and then, once he's fully inside me, he holds my breasts in his hand and pinches my nipples through the lace.

I gasp, the breath stolen from my lungs, but the intensity of the pleasure flooding my body. I'm weak with him, weak for him. My eyes clench shut, I throw my head back, giving in to everything this can be, everything this always has been. Everything it will be.

I move the cups down and thrust my chest forward, and he sucks my nipple into his mouth. The heat and wetness, the clamp of his teeth over my tender skin, sends me sailing, riding a wave of pleasure.

I rock hard against his cock, riding him, working my hips back and forth so hard I can hear the scrape of the thigh-highs against his legs.

If it bothers him, he's going with it, because he's sucking my tits like a meal and bouncing his hips up and down to match the pace of my grinding. I wrap my fingers behind his neck and pull his face closer, harder, riding and riding, chasing the bliss of release until I feel the tremble, the tightening.

"Fuck." I gasp, and then I stiffen, every muscle in my body tight in anticipation of the crash that takes over. I shudder and shake, and I can't stop the moans of absolute bliss that rocket past my lips. "Fuck, I'm coming. Oh God."

I scream through it, trembling all over. As soon as I still, dropping my head against Benny's shoulder, he puts his hands on my waist and fucks me while I'm boneless on top of him.

He writhes beneath me, lifting me up and slamming me back down on his cock. It feels so good. I feel myself losing control again, the tension building, the pleasure so overwhelming that another orgasm hits me, draining me of every ounce of strength. I'm floppy now, my face against Benny's bare chest, his cock pumping hard as he, too, comes with reckless moans and a fierceness that takes his breath away.

We collapse beside each other on the bed, panting, sweaty, our hair wild. He rolls onto his side, and I settle between his arms. I chuckle when he lifts a thigh and locks it over mine, covering me in heavy limbs.

"Is this your way of keeping me from leaving?" I tease.

"Is it working?" he asks.

I draw in a deep breath and close my eyes. "You don't have to keep me to have me," I say, my words blurry with sleep. "I love you, Benny. I love you too."

And saying it doesn't feel like too much.

It doesn't feel like too soon.

It feels right because I know it's true.

CHAPTER 19
WILLOW

FLORIDA IS a lot warmer than Ohio in November. I shrug out of the wool pea coat I wore on the plane and drag a roller bag behind me. I'm going to need cooler clothes where I'm going, but I don't want to confront the Kincades sweating like I ran a marathon to get here.

Since Audrina wouldn't answer my calls, I figured the only way to get some answers was to do what any stalker in pursuit of information would do. I show up at Pancake Circus. The original location. After checking in to a hotel for my one-night stay, I call a rideshare and text Benny.

Me: Wish me luck.

He sends back three thumbs-up emojis within seconds.

The rideshare picks me up at the front of the hotel, and I watch the landscape roll by on the short drive. The driver doesn't say much until we pull into the parking lot.

"Great place," he grumbles, not sounding at all happy. "Best eats in town."

I smile and thank him for the ride. If there's one thing that unites people, it's good food.

The parking lot of Pancake Circus is packed. The faded neon sign and the obvious signs of disrepair just add to the charm of the place. I'm again reminded why we picked this restaurant. An amazing menu. A bit of a gimmicky concept, but memorable. I just hope they don't kick me out or call the police. I've got Jessa on standby in case I need someone to wire bail money.

When I get to the door, I see a hand-lettered sign taped to it. "Closed for private event. Tickets required."

I pull open the door and am greeted by a handsome young guy. "Hi," he says brightly. "Thanks so much for coming. Are you here for the fundraiser or the restaurant?" He gives me a warm smile. "In case you missed the sign, we're closed for the day. But we'll open back up tomorrow for regular business."

"Uh…" I scramble to figure out the right thing to say. I want to get to the bottom of this, but I don't know if I should be here if there's a private event. "I was hoping to talk to Audrina Kincade," I say, looking around as though I might see her just standing around. "Do you know if she's here?"

"Of course," he says. "She's running the event. Are you a friend?" he asks. "I have a short list of people who have complimentary tickets. I can just check…"

Two other people have come up from behind me, so I step aside. "Why don't you go ahead," I say, waving them past. "I need to get out my debit card."

I listen while the people behind me pay for entry to the fundraiser. I luck out because while the younger woman pays, the older woman nods to me. "Do you know John Kincade?" she asks.

I nod, because I do. That's Audrina's grandfather. The man who opened Pancake Circus. "Not very well personally," I admit. "But professionally, yes."

The woman shakes her head slowly. "It's such a shame. They're such wonderful people." She leans in close to me. "I can't imagine losing everything like that. And you know how hard it is to deal with insurance companies these days."

I have no idea what she's talking about, but I nod and then step back into line. I hand the young man at the hostess stand my debit card and pay for a ticket. "Can you tell me how the family is doing?" I ask, not sure what I should say. I want to know what happened, but I'm afraid if I just come out and ask it, he won't sell me the ticket, won't let me in. That seems ridiculous, though. This is a fundraiser, so they should let in anyone willing to pay for a ticket. "And what really happened?" I add.

The young man runs my card and hands me a paper wristband. I peel the sticky backing and put the thing around my wrist while he explains.

"It's so sad, but they are so lucky nothing worse happened," he says, his voice sincerely distraught. "Mr. Kincade's wife accidentally started a kitchen fire in their home. She was able to get out safely, but they lost everything." He shakes his head. "They have insurance, but there's an investigation and a lot of delays and paperwork. And just the emotional side. Jeanine just turned eighty, and John is, I think, eighty-four now. They've lived in their home for over fifty years. And everything is gone overnight."

"Oh my gosh," I say. "But they are okay? No one was hurt."

He shakes his head. "No, thank goodness. Jeanine was in the hospital for a day or two being treated for minor burns and to make sure her diabetes was under control, but she's fine. Their church asked if they would close the restaurant for just one day to let people come and make donations to help the family with small expenses until the insurance money comes in."

I nod and thank him, then let him get on to checking in other people. Once I get inside the restaurant, the mood is a lot lighter. Food is out on long buffet tables, and people are talking and laughing, sharing memories and snacking on staples from the Pancake Circus menu. I make my way through the crowd and see Jeanine and John Kincade. They are sitting together at a booth, holding hands. They are smiling, but it's obvious the strain they are under.

People are coming up to them, chatting and leaving cards and envelopes on the table. The whole scene is surreal, and I feel like an intruder in a place I don't belong. I didn't bring my checkbook, and I don't know if there's another way to make donations, but I don't have to wait long before the sound of a microphone coming on draws all eyes to the center of the room.

"Hey, everyone." A young man holds the mic, and his smile lights up the Kincades' faces. "As most of you here know, I'm Nathan Kincade, John and Jeanine's great-nephew. I just wanted to thank you all for coming. As you know, my uncle John and aunt Jeanine have been staples of this community for over fifty years. In this time of personal struggle, our family has come together, but I think I speak for all of us when I say the show of support from the community has been overwhelming."

There are some claps and cheers from the crowd at that.

Nathan continues. "All the food and drinks have been donated for today's event, and my uncle's kitchen staff and servers have donated their time off the clock to serve and clean, so every penny of whatever you donate today will go right to John and Jeanine to help them cover any expenses they have until they have help from the insurance company." Nathan points to a man in the crowd. "No pressure, Don. But, yes, I'm looking at you."

Don holds his hands over his heart, and the crowd laughs.

"Don's my uncle's insurance agent. But we know, Don. You're not the one who writes the checks."

"But I would." Don, much quieter than Nathan without a microphone, still manages to be heard as he says, "I would if I could."

By the time the laughter dies down, Nathan is pointing to a bunch of unusual artwork that's hanging on the walls. "And for those of you who don't know her, talented textile artist Annie Hancock has donated some amazing pieces to be auctioned off. If you want to bid on a piece, just put your name down and the amount you want to bid on the sheet by the artwork itself." Nathan puts a hand over his heart. "Annie is a longtime customer of Pancake Circus and is just one of the hundreds of people like you all here today who have stepped up and contributed in a show of support for John and Jeanine."

When the applause dies down, Nathan again encourages everyone to eat and drink and expresses thanks on behalf of the family. As soon as he sets the microphone down, I make my way through the crowd and put a hand on his elbow. He turns to me with a warm smile.

"Hi," he says. "Thank you so much for coming."

"I'm so, so sorry that this has happened," I say. "I wonder if you could tell me if Audrina is here. I was hoping to just say a few words to her and then be on my way."

"Of course," he says. "Last I saw her, she was in the kitchen supervising. Let me get her for you."

To my shock, he doesn't ask who I am or what I want. I wouldn't be surprised, though, if this has been happening all day. People showing up wanting to express support and share condolences.

Nathan returns a few minutes later with Audrina close on his heels. The moment she sees me, her nostrils flare and her eyes narrow. "What are you doing here?" she demands.

Nathan looks from her to me, and for a second, I'm afraid she's going to make a scene. "I'm so sorry about this," I say. "Can I please have two minutes of your time? Then I promise, I'll leave, and you'll never see me again."

Nathan looks at his cousin, but she just points back toward the kitchen. "Cover for me?" she asks. Then she glares at me. "This won't take long."

I feel like an absolute asshole as I follow a storming Audrina through the crowded restaurant to a small door marked with a sign that reads *Office*. She yanks open the door and waits until I'm inside. She closes the door behind us but then stands by the door, her arms crossed over her chest.

"You shouldn't be here," she says, her voice accusing. "How dare you show up like this? What the hell do you want?"

I wish I could hug her, tell her I'm so sorry for what they are going through, but I only have a few seconds to get this out before she's no doubt going to send me packing. I say what I came to say quickly.

"Audrina, I had no idea this was happening today, or I never would have shown up. Since you wouldn't take my calls, I took a chance and flew down here. All I want is to talk to you. I think I have a solution that can get you out of the Star Falls situation and all of us out of an expensive legal mess. Can you give me five minutes, please?"

She looks stunned but then peeks at her watch. "Okay," she relents. "Five minutes."

She takes a seat at an old metal desk that is covered with papers and envelopes. She motions for me to sit, so I pull out a very old, well-worn wooden chair and perch on the edge of it.

"I don't want to assume, but it looks like you maybe

wanted out of the Star Falls location because of the fire?" I phrase it as a question.

She lowers her chin and nods. "Yeah," she says. "But my grandparents don't know about that yet. After they lost everything, they moved temporarily into my parents' house. We thought after Grandma got checked out by the doctor that she was okay, but…" She blinks fast. "Physically, they're okay. Emotionally?" She shakes her head. "Have you ever experienced a house fire?"

"No," I say, silently thankful that I have not. "But I imagine it's absolutely devastating."

Audrina nods. "Fifty years of treasured heirlooms. Clothes and pictures, toys and letters." Her voice breaks. "I know it's just stuff, but some stuff can't be replaced. Some stuff carries meaning. And for my grandma…" She sighs. "She blames herself. She feels like she destroyed our family's history. Our legacy." She meets my eyes. "I can't leave them, Willow. Two years ago, I thought striking out on my own and doing my own thing would be an amazing adventure. Now?"

She leans back in her chair, opens a desk drawer, and pulls out a box of tissues. She dabs at her eyes. "My grams could have been hurt or worse in that fire. I can't leave them. Can't spend the remaining years we have together so many miles away."

"Changing your mind is not a basis for getting out of a contract," I say, nodding. "I'm so sorry. You probably feel trapped."

She looks at me suspiciously. "I did, still do." She wrinkles up the tissue in her hand. "My lawyer told me there is no way out of the Culinary Capital contract.

Everything is legit, which is why they signed off on it in the first place. I told them they had to find a way out, so we filed the injunction. I know I can't get out of the deal for good, but my lawyers said they can delay things for at least one year."

She tosses the shredded tissue into a small trash bin by the desk and stares at me. "So, if you're here to get to me to change my mind, it won't happen. I'll give you the money you spent on the ticket to get in here, and you can go."

She stands up and looks like she's going to storm out when I hold up a hand. "Please, Audrina. Wait. I told you I thought I had a solution. Can you hear me out? Please?"

She looks me over skeptically but eventually nods. "All right."

We talk for the next forty-five minutes. I feel terrible taking her away from the event, but if we can sort this out now, it will be the solution to both of our problems. To the problems of a whole lot of people.

I answer all of her questions and ask a bunch of my own. We disagree about a lot, and at times, we raise our voices so loud, I'm worried that someone from the event will hear. But by the time I have the information I need, we're on calm, if not friendly, ground.

Now, I just need to convince my boss that this will work.

I make my way through the noisy crowd at Pancake Circus, nodding to Nathan as I show myself out. My first instinct is to text Benny, so while I wait for the rideshare to take me back to my hotel, I send him a message.

Me: What do you think about me sticking around in Star Falls? Like for good?

Instead of a text back, my phone rings.

"Are you serious?" he asks. "What's going on? How'd it go in Florida?"

"Well, I'm still here," I tell him. "I'm headed up to see Jessa tomorrow morning. But so far, so good. I'm cautiously optimistic that I can make this work."

"Who do I have to bribe?" he asks. "Because if it means you staying in Star Falls…"

I grin. "Hopefully it won't come to under-the-table deals," I laugh. "There are going to be so many lawyers looking this deal over…" I sigh. "It's scary, Benny."

"What part?" he asks. "The lawyers? Talking to your boss?"

All of it, I think. Commitment. Giving up the familiar. Putting myself out there in such a big way that I realistically don't know if I can ever come back from this decision.

As if reading my silence, Benny says, "All of it?"

I laugh. "Yeah, honestly. All of it. How's Mags?"

"Good," he says. "She's a fucking genius with spreadsheets and shit. Honestly, babe, I should have asked for help years ago. I feel like an asshole, seeing how much she got done in only one morning. One fucking morning."

"Old dogs can learn new tricks," I say, stepping off the curb as my rideshare shows up.

"Yeah, but this old dog is younger than you, babe," he reminds me.

"We going there?" I ask him.

"I am completely, totally, head over heels excited about having you in every way possible," he croons, his voice curling around my ears like a song. "When you coming home, babe? I miss you already."

"A week," I tell him. "I don't think I'll need much longer."

"Send me nudes every night to hold me over?" he asks.

I burst out laughing and wave at the rideshare driver who looks up at me in the rearview mirror. "I have to go," I tell Benny. "But I will send what you asked for."

"Yesss," he hisses. "I knew I loved you. Bye, babe."

"Bye, Benny."

As I end the call, I look behind us at the enormous faded sign for Pancake Circus as it grows smaller the farther away we drive. Then I look out the window, settling back in my seat. This driver is a lot chattier than the last.

"Did you go to the Kincades' fundraiser?" the woman asks. "Terrible tragedy. Such a good family."

I nod. "It is, and yes," I say. "They are a good family. The very best."

I stare out the window the rest of the way to my hotel. Unlike most trips I take, I'm not chatting up the driver. Not anxious to learn about the local food scene, the cuisine, the weather. My mind is on other places. Like the place I'm going to start calling home.

Five days later, I hug Jessa goodbye from the ottoman where I've been sitting with her since I arrived. I place a hand on her belly and wish the little guy a long and happy stay in his mama's belly.

"I'm so glad you visited," Jessa says, tears already falling down her cheeks. "God, I wish you could stay. I'll give you half this kid. We can be like those friends who adopt a baby and raise it together. Co-parents."

I wipe the tears from my cheeks and then hand her a tissue. "I would," I tell her. "In fact, if you'd asked me six months ago, I might have even said yes."

"Damn that sexy chef who stole your heart. Platonic co-parent homewrecker, that's what he is." Jessa rubs a hand over her belly. "You could have all this," she says wistfully. "Diaper blowouts and spit-up. Instead, you chose orgasms and great food. I just don't get it."

"Come visit me?" I ask her. "I know it will be hard with the baby, but I don't want to lose touch."

I'm getting emotional now. So much is changing so fast, not only in my life, but in Jessa's.

"How the hell would we lose touch? Our whole friendship, except for the one year you lived here, has happened over video. You think I'm going to forget how to video chat once I have a kid?" She pushes her long, dark hair back from her face. I've been washing it in a basin every day since I arrived because she really struggles to get up and stand in the shower. I've done so much to take care of her while I've been visiting, but now that I'm leaving, I realize how much she won't have and will have to do without when I'm gone. I think about all the millions of moments I've lost not being physically present with the people I love, always on the road, always moving on to the next adventure.

"I'll come visit you too," I tell her. "You're a priority, and I want this baby to know who his other mother is."

"Oh no." Jessa shakes her head. "Your co-parental rights have already been terminated. You get to be the cool aunt, though."

"I can handle that."

Jessa's mom comes in to let me know the car is here to take me to the airport. I kneel on the carpet and wrap my arms around Jessa. "I love you," I tell her through tears. "And I'm so happy for you. You're the best mom and the best friend."

"I'm so proud of you," Jessa whispers through her tears. "You are settling down, but you're not settling, Willow. I think you're finally making your own happy ending." She releases me and pats her belly. "I made mine. Now go on and get yours. And video chat me when you get to Chicago."

I kiss her, hug her two more times, and make Jessa's mom promise to call me the minute she goes into labor. Then I climb into another car and head to yet another airport. I'm off to try to convince Theresa and Rosemarie Ginetti to let me take the biggest risk of my career yet.

CHAPTER 20
BENITO

ONE YEAR LATER...

"Pops. Ma. Would you hurry up?" I nervously check my phone for the time. Today is the grand opening, and I need to be in two places at once. "Ma!" I holler again, but this time, I stop, images of my parents getting it on flashing through my mind. "Oh, for fuck's sake. I'm leaving," I call. "Don't you dare come down here unless you're fully dressed."

The door to the basement opens, and my pops comes up into the dining room, chuckling. "I really scarred you for life, eh, son?" He's wearing dress pants and a nice shirt, his glasses low on his nose. "I was trying to print out the receipt you sent me just in case your contractor needs it."

I soften the edges of my voice, relieved that I did not, once again, interrupt my parents' coitus. "Thank God," I tell him. "But don't worry. Mags handled all that yesterday. We've got this under control. I just need you guys to come with me."

Ma comes practically tumbling down the stairs, a pair of heels in her hand. "What's all the hollering about?" she asks. "Are we late? Benny, I thought we had tons of time?"

I kiss Ma and take the heels from her so she can grab her phone and purse. "We do, but I want to get there early for Willow. Come on. I need you guys to get moving."

My parents trade looks but don't argue. We head out to my SUV, and I hear Ma asking my dad, "Why again do we have to drive with Benny? Why can't we take our truck?"

"It's a surprise, Ma," I holler, unlocking the SUV.

On the drive over, my parents talk, but my mind is racing. Pancake Circus died a year ago. The dream of it and the reality. Willow went to Chicago to try to convince her bosses to let the Kincade family out of the deal. Willow offered to take Audrina's place. To stay in Star Falls and run the restaurant, while Audrina stayed on as a consultant, allowing her to stay in Florida with her family.

But between the lawyers and the Ginetti sisters, that deal was a no-go. But Willow wouldn't give up.

She went full throttle into the problem, arguing why it would be better for the Ginettis to terminate the deal and let the Kincades out than to litigate and waste a lot of money and time. After a lot of legal wrangling and after the Kincades agreed to pay a crapload of money to repay a portion of the expenses it would require for Culinary Capital to start over, the old deal was canceled.

No more Pancake Circus in Star Falls. But a new deal was signed in its place.

Willow Watkins quit her position as COO of Culinary Creations. And she entered into an agreement with Culinary Creations as a client. Willow is now the proud owner of her very own breakfast and brunch restaurant here in Star Falls. Her consulting executive chef, yours truly, was paid a handsome sum to help create an original menu since the Kincades did not want to license any of their recipes as part of the termination agreement.

Thanks to the generous consulting fee I received, I was able to give Mags a nice raise, pay for a new roof over at Benito's, and buy a couple of extras. Both of which I'm hoping to unveil today.

We pull into the pristine blacktop of the Pancake Paradise parking lot. Willow's car is already there, along with a dozen others. She picked a weekday to host a friends and family only soft open of the restaurant, so the crowd is small. But I see a familiar face pushing a stroller in circles in the parking lot, so I tell my parents to join me as soon as they can.

I run across the lot and give a big hug to Willow's best friend, Jessa.

"I'm so glad you could make it," I tell her, hugging her tight.

"You promised me ravioli," she says, hugging me hard. "What woman could resist that?"

I bend down to little Walker, who is red-faced and squirming in his seat. "Have you seen Auntie Willow yet, little man?"

"Oh yes," Jessa says. "We came out here because I need a break. I'm looking at those two bonus grandparents for some relief."

Jessa points to Ma and Pops, who already have their arms out to pick up Walker.

"Good," I say. "I'll see you inside."

I turn to head inside the restaurant, patting my phone as it vibrates with a text.

Mags: It's all ready. And it's covered, but I saw it, Benny. Fuck, it's beautiful.

Just seeing the words, I know my life is about to change even more.

Me: Love it, thank you. C u soon.

Inside Pancake Paradise, I'm shocked to see my whole family is already here. I'm amazed to see everyone not only present and on time but looking as excited as I feel.

I make the rounds of the room, hugging Franco and Chloe, who stand together holding hands, Chloe beaming like today is her grand opening and not Willow's. That's what I love so much about Chloe. She's so, so sweet and so loving. Her peanut butter crisps are on display on the front counter—another way we were able to pay forward the good fortune as part of the deal with Culinary Creations. Chloe licensed her recipe to Willow to include the amazing cookies on the menu.

"Happy for you, bro," Franco says, clapping me on the back. "It's a great day for our family."

I shush him because God knows my fucking brother and his big mouth will blab before Ma and Pops see the surprise. "Thanks, man," I say, and then I point to Chloe. "Don't let him fuck this up, okay?"

She laughs and loops her arm through Franco's, then silences him with a kiss.

"That'll work," I say, heading over to Gracie next.

"Not bad," Gracie says, a huge smile on her face. "Not bad at all."

"Not bad," I mock her, repeating her words. I point to the walls vibrantly painted with murals in each section of the huge restaurant. Incredibly detailed palm trees and flowers cover the walls, and in the kid-friendly play area, life-sized monkeys, zebras, parrots, and elephants come to life, thanks to Gracie's art. "Couldn't have done this without you, sis."

I hug Gracie and hold her tight. Ryder, Gracie's husband, is sitting next to his buddy, Austin. We chat about Gracie's artwork until I feel a slap on the back of my head.

"Hey, dumbass." I turn to face Vito, who's looking at me with a goofy grin plastered on his face. "When's breakfast?"

"Oh my God, man." I give him a punch to the ribs, then a brotherly hug. Eden and Junie are over in the kids' area, playing with Gracie's three kids. I wave and blow them kisses, relieved when I see Ma and Pops wandering over with little Walker. When I turn back, Gracie is introducing Jessa to Austin.

We're all here.

Everybody but one.

I walk back into the kitchen and find her. Willow's

silky blond hair is up in a bun, and she's wearing a chef's coat over a dress as she talks with her staff.

"Remember, everyone," she says, clasping her hands in front of her chest, "I am so, so happy to have you all on my team. Let's have some fun and make some great food."

When she turns to leave and she sees me, her face lights up. She practically runs for me and throws herself against my chest.

"Nervous?" I ask, kissing the top of her head. Even though we already had this talk when we woke up this morning, I know how different it is to have hungry stomachs waiting and a crew at the ovens ready to go.

"Happy," she says. "Surprisingly un-nervous." She rises on her toes and whispers in my ear. "A morning of orgasms definitely helped chill me out."

I kiss her lightly. "Just doing my part."

The lease on Willow's condo is up in two weeks, and she's decided to move in with me. We both love the building, and Jessa and Walker are going to crash in her place while they're here to celebrate the soft open. The last year has flown by, but if one thing hasn't changed, it's how I feel about Willow. If anything, I love her and want her as much, if not more, than I did a year ago.

So much so, in fact, that I've made a few changes of my own.

Our family and friends order off the menu, give Willow feedback on the dishes, and congratulate the chefs on the opening. Everything is delicious, and while there are a few minor delays, some cold toast and warm milk that need addressing, Pancake Paradise is ready for business.

By the time we're done eating, my family all heads out, pretending they have to get to work and other places. My folks stay back since they are riding with me to our next destination. But before we go, I need a minute alone with Willow.

I see Mags walk in, and I wave her over.

"I know you want to get to cleaning and debriefing with your staff, but I asked Mags to come by to supervise and train." Willow looks confused, but she's nodding. "Can I talk to you in your office for a second?"

She gives me a look but agrees and heads back to the small, perfectly orderly space that is her new office. As soon as she shuts the door, I pull her into my arms.

"Baby," I say. "I don't want to take away from your big day, but I have two surprises for you." I chuckle. "Well, I guess depending on how the first one goes, there may only be one surprise, but we'll see."

She looks at me, puzzled, but as soon as I get down on one knee, her mouth drops open.

"Willow, you're the love of my life, and you know how much I love my restaurant." I laugh, and she covers her mouth, her eyes glossy with tears. "The day I met you was the day I knew you were different. No other woman sucked my dick in the shower like you did."

"Benny." She's crying now, a smile on her face, and pulls me to standing. "What are you doing?"

"I want you to marry me, babe. Spend your life with me. Make amazing food, amazing memories, and even better orgasms." I lean down to kiss her. "If you tell people about this later…"

She is full-body cry-laughing now. "After what I've seen of your parents' sex life, I hardly think they'd be shocked."

"Oh," I tell her, then reach into the pocket of my jacket to pull out a small velvet box. "Also, I got you a ring."

She's doubled over now with laughter. "At least you didn't propose with a plate of ravioli."

"Would that have worked?" I ask. "Because it would've been a whole lot cheaper."

"Give me that," she says, taking the box from me. She opens it to reveal an oval-shaped diamond with two star-shaped diamond clusters on either side. "Oh, Benny."

I take the box from her and slide the ring over her finger. "I hope this means you're saying yes, because if not, the next part of the surprise is going to really suck."

"Yes," she says, throwing herself into my arms. "Yes, yes."

I pick her up and swing her around, then set her on her feet and take her hand.

"Okay, we can celebrate later. Next surprise."

I pull her from the office into the restaurant, where my parents are waiting for us. "Ma, Pops," I say as we approach them. "I have two more surprises for you…" I hold out Willow's hand, where her ring sparkles on her finger. "First, you're getting another daughter."

My ma squeals—I'm talking shrieks—and grabs Willow in the tightest hug ever. Pops has to break in between the tears and the rocking to congratulate Willow, but I'm already headed for the door. "Come on, come on. Next surprise. Let's go."

Ma, Pops, and Willow look confused, but they follow me to the SUV. They chatter among themselves, all three of them together in the backseat while I make the quick drive over to my restaurant. Well, it was my restaurant. I find my own eyes stinging as I pull into the parking lot. My entire family and all our friends have made the trip here for the second surprise. My whole staff, Sassy, Jasmine, Rita, Carla, Duncan— everybody but Mags, who agreed to hold down the fort at Pancake Paradise for a couple of hours so I could orchestrate this whole day. She'll celebrate with us later. She knows I couldn't have done any of this without her.

In addition to our family, I invited my ma's friends, Carol and Bev, so we could all be together for this special announcement.

Once we're all together, gathered in the parking lot of my restaurant, I take Willow's hand and drag her to the front of the crowd. I don't have a mic, but I don't need one. Everyone's fallen silent, waiting and watching.

"Everybody. Thanks for being willing to go along with the surprise. I have excellent news." I hold up Willow's hand. "She said yes."

Jessa screams from beside Ryder's friend Austin, and I have to wait until the hugs and tears and congratulations die down before I can get to the next part.

I wipe a tear from my own eye, my emotions really

getting to me now that everyone is here and the moment has finally come.

"First of all," I say, "I want to thank you all, my family and friends, who have supported me throughout the years I've owned Benito's. I've missed a lot of time with a demanding mistress—" I motion toward the restaurant "—but it only prepared me, I hope, to be the best possible husband to this angel."

I kiss the back of Willow's hand and have to pause to collect myself. I wipe yet another tear from my cheek as I turn to face the cord keeping the tarp covering the Benito's sign in place. When I give the cord a yank, the tarp falls away, revealing a brand-new sign. The name on the sign is no longer Benito's. The sign reads Bianchi's Family Eatery.

My ma immediately bursts into tears, and Willow gasps.

My voice cracks a little as I continue. "Over the last year, I've had a lot of help making my business better than it has ever been. And it's more than I ever thought it could be. Thanks to all of you, for all the work you've done, the love you've shown me, and the time you've spent even just eating my food, Benito's is better than ever. And this seemed like the perfect time to make a change that reflects what I believe is Benito's future. A future more focused on family. On the beauty and love that we share. Of every blessing and good thing we have because we have one another."

There's not a sound as my family and friends look at me, their expressions ranging from shocked to proud.

I clap my hands. "Well, that's it, people. A new sign. And I'm engaged. Let's celebrate."

Willow laces her fingers through mine and lifts up on her toes to kiss me. The next hour passes in a blur of congratulations, well-wishes, expressions of love, and a hell of a lot of teasing about what I did with the old sign, the one with my name on it.

Truth be told, I threw it out. Because if I've learned anything over the past few years, it's that there is no me without the people I love. Without my siblings and their spouses and kids, who bring my life such richness. Without my parents, whose unfailing love for their family is the foundation of every value I have. Without my friends and all the people in the Star Falls community who make the life I have and the work I do so joyful.

And last but not least, Willow.

She may have taken a long road to find me, but nothing we each had to go through was too much to bear, too much to experience. Because now that we have each other, our work, and so much love in our lives, this is not the end of our story.

It's just the beginning.

LOVE SIGNED PAPERBACKS?

Visit *chelleblissromance.com* for signed paperbacks
and book merchandise.

THE MEN OF INKED FAMILY SAGA EBOOK COLLECTION

Join the Gallo family as their lives are turned upside down by irresistible chemistry and unexpected love.

Get the entire Men of Inked saga or other bundles by visiting chelleblissromance.com or your favorite retailer.

ABOUT THE AUTHOR

I'm a full-time writer, time-waster extraordinaire, social media addict, coffee fiend, and ex-history teacher. *To learn more about my books, please visit menofinked.com.*

Want to stay up-to-date on the newest
Men of Inked release and more?
Join my newsletter at *menofinked.com/news*

Join over 10,000 readers on Facebook in Chelle Bliss Books private reader group and talk books and all things reading. Come be part of the family!

See the Gallo Family Tree

Where to Follow Me:

facebook.com/authorchellebliss1

instagram.com/authorchellebliss

bookbub.com/authors/chelle-bliss

goodreads.com/chellebliss

tiktok.com/@chelleblissauthor

amazon.com/author/chellebliss

pinterest.com/chellebliss10

Don't Miss Out!

Join my newsletter for exclusive content, special freebies, and so much more. Click here to get on the list or visit **menofinked.com/news**

Do you want to have your very own **SIGNED paperbacks** on your bookshelf? Now you can get them! Tap here to check out Chelle Bliss Romance or visit **chelleblissromance.com** and stock up on paperbacks, Inked gear, and other book worm merchandise!

Join over 10,000 readers on Facebook in Chelle Bliss Books private reader group and talk books and all things reading. Tap here to come be part of the family or visit **facebook.com/groups/blisshangout**

Want to be the first to know about upcoming sales and new releases? Follow me on Bookbub or visit bookbub.com/authors/chelle-bliss

Made in the USA
Columbia, SC
05 September 2024

41826709R00178